This book belongs to:

....

....

MY BOOK OF

dragon

STORIES

MY BOOK OF

dragon

STORIES

Written by
NICOLA BAXTER

Illustrated by
ANDREW WARRINGTON

This is a Parragon Book
First published in 2000

Parragon
Queen Street House
4 Queen Street
Bath BA1 1HE, UK

Copyright © Parragon 2000

ISBN 0-75253-512-9

Produced for Parragon by
Nicola Baxter
PO Box 215
Framingham Earl
Norwich NR14 7UR

Designed by Amanda Hawkes

Printed in Italy

Contents

The Tiniest Dragon

Edward was a boy who didn't believe anything he was told. He always had to see for himself. It was partly because he was pretty clever and from an early age had realized that grown-ups say some very silly things to children.

"Here comes the big orange plane," his mother used to coo, swooping a large spoonful of carrots towards his mouth when he was a toddler and refusing to eat anything except bananas and yogurt.

Edward looked at her in disgust. "It isn't," he said, and shut his mouth firmly.

"Oh Edward! You're hurting poor Mr. Bear," his father used to say, when Edward tried out his new plastic hammer on Mr. Bear's nose.

"He isn't alive, you know," said Edward coldly.

When Edward was older, things became even more difficult. At Grandma's birthday party, when she giggled and told him she was thirty-nine, Edward's "You've got to be joking!" rather spoilt the festive atmosphere.

Later, at school, Edward's teachers found him hard work. He always wanted proof of anything they said, and that could be difficult.

"How do you know there's nothing growing on the moon?" he asked. "Have you ever been there?"

"No, of course not," replied the teacher, "but other people have. Their reports say that there is nothing at all growing on the moon."

"People often don't tell the truth," said Edward grimly. "How do you know you can trust them?"

"You'll just have to take my word for it, Edward," replied his teacher. "Now we must move on."

Edward's questions, she knew from experience, could take up the whole lesson. It was very difficult.

As time went on, Edward found there were not many subjects that he felt happy about. Maths was fine. He could work out the problems and feel confident that everything was true—and provable. Music was okay, too. He could hear with his own ears if something sounded right. History and geography were minefields until a new teacher explained to him one day about *evidence*. After that, Edward began to enjoy the idea of using real things to show what was true. He was upset when Grandma refused to lend him her birth certificate to back up his family history project, but Granddad was more helpful.

"Of course, he's much older than me," said Grandma.

The subject that Edward found most difficult was English. Time and again, he was asked to make up a story about something

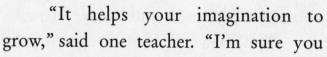

"But what's the point?" asked Edward.

"It helps your imagination to grow," said one teacher. "I'm sure you make up lots of wonderful stories in your head, Edward. We just want to hear some of them."

"No, I don't," said the boy. "Why would I want to do that? It wouldn't be true. You can't trust made-up things."

"Well, in a way you're right," replied the teacher, "but you can enjoy them. And sometimes they're true in other ways. If you read a story about a boy being afraid of a ghost, for example, it doesn't mean that there really are ghosts or that there really was a boy who was afraid of them. It means that people are often afraid of things they don't really understand. That's true, even if the story isn't, do you see?"

Edward looked unconvinced. "I'll write a diary instead," he said. "It will be a sort of story, but it will be true."

The teacher sighed and agreed.

One term, Mrs. Martin the teacher announced that instead of writing lots of different stories, each pupil would write one long story, like a proper book. They would write a chapter each week. At the end, a real author, who lived nearby, would come and read the books and award prizes for the most imaginative. All the children were very excited—except one, of course.

"I don't know why I have to bother," he said. "Mine isn't going to be imaginative at all. I'm going to write a diary again."

"Well, if that is what you feel happy doing, that will be fine," said his teacher, but it didn't make *her* feel happy. For the past year she had read dozens of "stories" from Edward, all of them in diary form, and they were, frankly, desperately boring.

"Today I got up at seven thirty. I had cereal and an orange for breakfast. It was raining when I set off for school, so I wore my raincoat. I looked at my gauge and saw that two centimetres of rain had fallen overnight. I told Mrs. Martin at school, but she didn't seem interested. James Prothero stole my pencil. We had cheese salad and apple pie for lunch. I got A$^+$ for my maths homework. It was still raining when I went home."

Mrs. Martin thought of having to read a whole book full of this kind of thing and shuddered, but there was no alternative. Edward would only write about things he knew were true, and that was the end of it.

But Edward's life was about to change in the most extraordinary way. That evening, after he had eaten his supper (and recorded every mouthful in his new "story" diary), Edward sat down at the desk in his room to do his homework. It was maths, which he enjoyed, so it was some time before he noticed little puffs of smoke coming from his pencil-case.

Edward looked down at it in horror. He had learnt about fire safety in school. His pencils must be on fire! He knew he shouldn't open the zip, in case the fire spread, so he ran into the bathroom, filled a tumbler with water, and threw it over the pencil-case, first moving his maths homework well out of the way. The smoke stopped at once, but something even odder happened. The pencil-case began to splutter.

Edward watched it in amazement. With each splutter (and what sounded very like a cough) the pencil-case gave a little jump. Summing up the possibilities in his mind, Edward could come to only one conclusion. There was something (very small) inside.

The more he thought about it, the surer Edward became that what was inside his pencil-case must be a mouse. It could have crept in at school and been chewing his pencils ever since. Maybe it wasn't smoke he had seen. Maybe it was puffs of sawdust or something like that. Edward didn't much like the idea of a mouse running about in his bedroom, so he carried the dripping case carefully into the bathroom, shut the door firmly (and locked it), and put the jiggling pencil-case down in the sink. Then, very, very slowly, he pulled back the zip.

It wasn't a mouse, although it was about that size. Mice, Edward knew, are not green and orange with wings. It must, he thought, be a bat—some kind of fruit-eating bat from a tropical country. But just as Edward was thinking of going back to his room to look up the creature in his nature encyclopedia, the animal gave a final splutter and began to smoke. I don't mean that it had a cigarette or anything horrible like that. I mean that little puffs of smoke began coming out of its nose.

Edward's mind was racing. He seemed to remember some story from school about a legend that salamanders live in fires. But salamanders didn't have wings, he knew. And anyway, that was just a story. It wasn't *true*. It was because salamanders often live in dead logs, and when these are thrown on to a fire, they run out. This little creature wasn't run-

ning anywhere. It looked perfectly happy.
Edward hurried out of the bathroom,
shutting the door carefully behind him,
and retrieved his magnifying glass from
his room. Locked safely in the bathroom
again, he approached the creature once
more. This time, he could make a proper,
scientific identification.

It was a while before Edward could
believe what his eyes were telling him.
Using the magnifying glass, he could see

that not only smoke but tiny flames were coming from the creature's nostrils. He could see that the green and orange skin was made up of tiny scales. He could see that it had a long tail with a forked bit on the end. In short, he could see that the tiny animal sitting quietly in the sink was not a mouse, or a fruit-bat, or a salamander. It was a dragon.

You know, and I know, and Edward knew that dragons are not *real*, like cows and pigs are real. They are imaginary, like fairies and goblins and unicorns. But Edward also knew that one of these entirely imaginary creatures was sitting in his bathroom sink. He needed to do some serious thinking—and fast!

You or I might have been puzzled about the whole thing. So puzzled that our brains refused to take in what we were seeing or to think slowly and sensibly about it afterwards. Edward, after a couple of minutes, found that the situation was surprisingly simple. How, he reasoned, did he know that there were no such things as dragons? He knew because books and teachers had told him so. Did he believe everything that he read in books or was told by teachers? No! Did he believe things he could see to be true with his own eyes? Definitely! There was no question about it. There was a tiny dragon in his bathroom. The only problem now was deciding what to do next.

"I wish," said Edward, thinking out loud, "that I knew what dragons like to eat. At least, I think that big dragons like to eat people, but what could this one manage?" He peered again at the creature.

"Mmmmmnnnng," said the dragon, with its mouth full. Clearly hungry, the dragon had answered the question itself by tucking into the soap. Although Edward was doubtful whether this was a nutritious meal for any reptile, the dragon itself seemed perfectly happy. Half a bar disappeared before it sat down with what sounded very like a burp. Edward, thinking that the creature must now be thirsty, turned on the cold tap so that just a little trickle came out of it.

At once, a tiny screeching came from the sink, and the dragon started to hop about in an agitated way. Edward bent down. It wasn't screeching. The dragon was talking, but in a very, very tiny voice.

"Turn it off! Turn it off!" it was squeaking. "Don't you know anything? Turn it off!"

Edward did as he was told. Then he leaned down again and asked, "Why?"

"Dragons *hate* water!" squealed the dragon. "It puts our flames out! And they're *so* difficult to light again. Which reminds me…"

"Oh," Edward knew what was coming. "I'm sorry about that," he said, "throwing the water over you, I mean. I thought my pencil-case was on fire."

"That was pretty silly," commented the dragon. "What on earth made you think that?"

"The smoke," said Edward sharply. He didn't take kindly to being told he was silly by a creature not much bigger than his nose. "*Your* smoke," he pointed out.

"Ah, well, I suppose I can see your point," said the dragon. "That could have been the explanation. But didn't it occur to you that it might be a dragon?"

"Of course not," replied Edward. "I didn't know dragons existed."

"Didn't know they existed? Our publicity of late has been shockingly bad," sighed the dragon. "But I know for a fact that there are dozens of children's stories with dragons in them. How could you possibly not know? Can't you read?"

"Of course I can!" Edward was even more indignant. "But those stories are made up. The things in them aren't true, you know."

"Really?" There was deep sarcasm in the dragon's tone. "So how do you explain me, then?"

Edward couldn't.

The dragon stayed with Edward for almost two months. He seemed to appear at odd times, but never when anyone else was around. It didn't occur to Edward not record his conversations with the dragon in his story-diary.

Those two months changed Edward's life. He had to think again about many things, such as whether you could believe what you read in books and what it really meant to say that something was true. He began to notice things he had never noticed before, such as the way that clouds sometimes looked like dragons and that there seemed to be a man smiling in the moon. He knew that the clouds weren't dragons and there was no man in the moon, but he understood now that it could be fun to think about things that only *seemed* to be true. His family, his teachers and his friends gradually found him much, much easier to be around. He liked them better, too.

Even so, Edward was amazed when his diary was chosen as "the story showing the most imagination" at the end of term. He was even more amazed by the pleasure that his success seemed to give everyone else. It was really nice. He liked it so much that he didn't notice until the next day that the dragon had gone—completely.

Edward searched for a long time. He even hunted in those places you'd rather not investigate, such as the darkest corners of the bathroom and inside his brother's trainers. There was no sign of the dragon.

For several weeks, Edward felt sure that from the corner of his eye he caught sight of little flickering flames and puffs of smoke. But however fast he turned around, they were never really there.

So the dragon had disappeared for ever. Nowadays, Edward is even happy about that. And on cold, frosty mornings, when his breath looks like little puffs of smoke, he wears a secret smile.

The Most Dangerous Dragon

Sometimes, when a cold wind whistled around the turrets of the castle, and the hunting dogs crowded close to the great fire, old Duncan Dobetter told stories to the youngsters of the court. His favourite subject was ... dragons.

"As you know, a dragon is always dangerous," Duncan would say, pulling his cloak closer about his shoulders, "but the dragon you should truly fear is the most dangerous dragon of all. He is the invisible dragon. He could be with us now, here in this hall, and we would never know until it was TOO LATE!"

Stefan Stinkle listened with interest. He had long been trying to think of a way of making his mark in the world. Dragon-slaying seemed a good option. Instant fame and certain wealth had a great deal of appeal. But did old Duncan know what he was talking about? Had he, for example, ever come face to face with a dragon himself?

"Let me tell you, young Stinkle," cried Duncan, "I've met more dragons than you've had hot flagons, which I hope at your age isn't very many. I'll tell you a story that will make your hair stand on end."

Stefan smirked. "Go on then," he said.

Duncan settled down near the fire and beckoned the youngsters, including young Stefan, to join him. When he spoke, his voice was dark and mysterious.

"When I was young," he said, "and you can wipe that expression off your face right away, young Stinkle—I *was* young once—my grandmother warned me that in every generation of our family at least one son was lost to a dragon. 'It has been that way with the Dobetters,' she said, 'since the beginning of time, and it will be that way for ever. I thought it was only fair to warn you, young Duncan, that your days are numbered.'"

"But why did it have to be you?" asked one of the lads. "Couldn't it have been a brother or a cousin?"

"It could," said Duncan, "if I had had any brothers or male cousins. But I didn't. I had seven sisters myself and more girl cousins than I could count. There were only two options. Either my parents had more children, or I met my doom."

"And did they?" Even Stefan Stinkle was getting interested. He had six sisters himself and experienced a certain fellow feeling for old Duncan.

"Yes, they did," said the old man. "They had four more children ... and they were all girls. Since it seemed that I would one day die at the claws of a dragon, I decided to find out all I could about the dreaded creature. I hoped that I would be able to use my wits to stave off the evil hour for as long as possible. I became, in a remarkably short time, an expert on the habits and habitats of every kind of dragon known to humankind. It was quite fascinating."

"Why?" asked Stinkle, thinking of his future career. "What is there to know?"

"Ah," old Duncan took another swig from his goblet. "There is a very great deal to know. Could you tell me, for example, how dragons are born?"

"Born? They're not born!" scoffed Stinkle. "They just *are* like mountains and music. Dragons are always hundreds of years old, aren't they?"

"Dragons who bother humans are usually hundreds of years old, yes," said Duncan, "but all dragons were young once. They hatch out of eggs, deep in the mountains."

"I've never heard of a dragon's egg," said another listener. "Why hasn't anyone ever seen one?"

"Because they are grey, like rocks, and very big. You have probably all seen them, but they just look like big, grey boulders to you."

The boys shuddered.

"How big are baby dragons?" they asked, frowning.

"About as big as a cow," replied the dragon expert. "But they are very shy. Their mothers keep them deep inside a cosy cave until they are ready to start rampaging about the countryside."

"What do they eat, deep inside the cave?" asked Stinkle. He wasn't sure he believed any of this.

"Anyone their mother brings back from her hunting trips," replied Duncan.

"*Anyone?* But don't they eat cows and sheep and rabbits and things, too?" asked Marku, the budding naturalist.

"Only if they are very hungry," said Duncan. "Humans are their preferred food. They particularly like people with red hair and long noses. You were saying, Stinkle?"

"Nothing," said Stefan, pulling down his helmet.

"I want to hear more of the story," said a boy. "You said that you had met dragons. What happened?"

"The very first dragon that I met was that very dangerous kind I mentioned at the beginning. He was invisible, but absolutely deadly."

"If he was invisible, how did you know he was there?" Stinkle was still unimpressed.

"Believe me, Stefan, when you are in the presence of a dragon, *you know*. At least, you know if you have your wits about you. It happened like this. I was walking through the woods one day when I began to notice a smell of burning. The air felt warmer, too, although the day was cold and the leaves of the trees shut out the sun. As I walked on, I noticed that patches of leaves and bits of tree trunks were black, as if they had been scorched. I should have known the truth then, but I didn't have the sense to see it. I just kept on walking."

"Could you hear the dragon?"

"No, the woods were strangely silent. That should have warned me, but it didn't. Not a single bird sang in the branches. There were no squirrels or little woodland creatures of any kind. I walked on in the eerie silence … into a thick and suffocating fog."

"A fog? Like the one that forms in the valley every morning?" asked one lad.

"Exactly like that," replied Duncan with a smile. "This fog swirled around me in a strange way. I kept thinking I could glimpse shapes and shadows on the path, but there was never anything there. And the fog was warm, too, not cold and clammy like most mists. It was the breath of the dragon, you see, curling around the trees and surrounding me. I still didn't know that it was a dragon, but I began to be very frightened. For one thing, I knew that I was completely lost."

"You should have marked the trees," said Stinkle. "Everyone knows that's what you should do if you can't find your way."

"Well, perhaps you are right," said Duncan, "but I've never seen how that could help. It wouldn't stop you walking in a circle, it would just mean that you would know if you were … walking in a circle, I mean. Anyway, I didn't do it, so it's neither here nor there. What I did do, which was a big mistake, was to call out for help."

"That's what I would have done," said one of the listeners, loyally.

"Thank you, Clarence. It did seem a good idea at the time. And only a few seconds later it seemed as if help had come. An old man appeared out of the fog, wearing a thick grey cloak with a hood over his eyes. One moment he wasn't there. The next, he sort of formed himself out of a thicker area of fog. At least, that's what it seemed like, but the light can play strange tricks with your eyes."

"But wasn't it spooky, if you couldn't see his face?" Clarence wasn't the bravest lad in the castle.

"I didn't think of that then," the old man explained. "I was just so glad to see another human soul. I ran towards him shouting out with delight. It was only when I reached him, and he raised his hooded head, that I saw his ghastly face."

"What was it like?" All the lads asked together.

"My words may have been a little misleading," said Duncan slowly, taking another drink from his goblet. "What was really terrifying was that there was no face. The figure in the dark robes had an even darker void where his face should have been."

"Did you run?" asked Clarence.

"My feet were rooted to the spot. Even if I had wanted to escape, my legs refused to move. And in any case, it didn't matter. In a second or two, the horrible figure in front of me began to dissolve into the mist. It seemed to swirl for a moment and then was gone."

"What a relief!" said Marku.

"In a way," replied Duncan, gazing into the dying embers of the fire, "but I suddenly felt more alone than I had ever

been in my life. And what happened next was even more frightening."

He sipped again from his goblet.

"Go on! Go on!" The boys were desperate to know what had happened.

"The mist began to thicken," said Duncan, holding one hand after another out to the fire as though he felt a chill deep in his bones. "And it suddenly became very, very hot. I could feel a burning on my neck and face as the swirling air licked at it."

"It was the dragon!" cried Clarence.

"Yes, but I still didn't know that. I only knew that I was absolutely terrified and that my thoughts were whirling so fast in my head that I couldn't think of a single sensible thing to do. In fact, I was a young lad then, so I'm not ashamed to tell you that tears were streaming down my face as I stood there."

"And then?" Stefan's tone was not sympathetic.

"I fell to my knees and clutched the trunk of the nearest tree," said Duncan. "To my horror, what I felt beneath my face and fingers was not the rough bark I was expecting, but smooth, shiny scales like the skin of a snake. That was when I knew for the first time that I was dealing with a dragon. I knew that the end had come."

Outside the castle, the wind howled. There was silence in the great hall, except for the sullen thud of a smouldering log shifting on the fire.

The boys looked up at old Duncan with open mouths.

"What happened? How did you escape?" they cried, gazing eagerly at the old man.

Only Stefan Stinkle had a look of something close to disdain on his face. More and more, he found himself doubtful about Duncan Dobetter's story. Worse still, he began to wonder if he had been right to consider a dragon-slaying career. Clearly, Duncan had escaped from the encounter he was now describing. And, if what he had said before was to be believed, it was not the only time he had met a dragon and survived. If a man like Duncan Dobetter—not particularly clever, or brave, or strong—could meet dozens of dragons and survive, it must be pretty easy. And something that anyone could do would never bring in the fame and riches that Stefan had planned for himself. As these things passed through his mind, he felt Duncan's eyes upon him, a peculiar expression on his aged face.

Duncan leaned down to fill his goblet from the flagon standing near the hearth. It was empty.

"Stefan," he said mildly, "my old throat is parched. I must have some more of the cook's devilish brew before I go on. Will you go down to the kitchens and fill the flagon for me?"

"Oh, why me?" whined Stefan at once. "Why can't one of the others go?" But something in the old man's face stopped him. Picking up the empty vessel, he set off reluctantly for the kitchens far below in the depths of the castle.

Now, I expect you know very well that medieval castles were not the most comfortable of places. They were dark, cold and draughty. There was no glass in the tiny slit-like windows. You either froze in the passages and stairways or almost suffocated in the smoke of the rooms with fires. The only positive thing to be said for living in a castle was that it was a whole lot better than sleeping under a hedge, which was the fate of most of the peasants living round about.

Stefan Stinkle's mind wasn't on peasants as he made his way down the steep, circular stone stairs. The treads were worn by many feet, and the flaming torches that burned on the walls were few and far between. It was hard enough to keep your footing at the best of times, but with freezing draughts whistling around your ears and a flagon pressed to your chest, it was harder than usual.

The flickering torches made weird shadows jump and twist on the walls. Stefan felt himself shivering, and not only from the cold. Who could know what was lurking around the next curve? Or what was creeping down the stairs behind him?

Never had Stefan been so glad to reach the warmth and noise of the kitchens, a place he usually hated. They were filled with the steamy smells of cooking food, cooling food and, in the darkest corners, rotting food. The cook, too, a huge man with hands like shovels, dressed in a greasy robe, was terrifying at the best of times. Tonight, though, he looked reassuringly normal and human.

Stefan filled the flagon and only turned once more towards the stairs with the greatest reluctance.

It was even worse going up than coming down. The flagon was heavier, and Stefan soon found himself panting as he climbed the uneven steps. His breathing sounded unnaturally loud in his ears. Once again he began to have strange fears.

Was that a sound, lower than the howling of the wind, sharper than his ragged breaths, just above in the darkness? Surely there had been more light on the way down? By the time Stefan rounded the final curve and saw ahead of him the open doorway of the great hall, he had worked himself up into a real panic. His mouth felt dry and his legs trembled.

His footsteps quickened as he saw the flickering orange light from the fire through the doorway. He had never felt so glad to see the rest of the lads before.

But the flagon-bearer hadn't taken three steps inside the room before he realized that something was wrong. Very wrong. Terrifyingly wrong.

The vast room was much smokier than he remembered. Warm, white tendrils of smoke were snaking across the floor, winding themselves around Stefan's legs and swirling up towards his face.

Surely the room had not been as hot as this either? After the cold stairway, the vast hall felt oppressive.

Stefan rubbed his eyes to peer through the smoke towards the fireplace. He could see now that there was only one figure, standing with its back towards him. Of the lads he had left behind, there was no sign. A cold trickle of fear ran down the boy's back. There was an odd silence in the room.

From the fireplace, Duncan spoke.

"Ah, Stefan Stinkle," he said in a voice that was deep and somehow dreadful,

"I wonder how much you have guessed of what has happened here today?"

Stefan found himself unable to answer, but his eyes must have shown that he understood only too well.

"Yes," said Duncan, "there are only three outcomes if a human meets a dragon. The human may kill the dragon. The dragon may kill the human. Or..."

Stefan found his voice. "Or the human becomes a dragon in human form," he whispered. "I didn't know... I mean I didn't..."

"Didn't you?" hissed Duncan. "Oh, I think you did, Stefan. As soon as I saw you, I knew what a very fine dragon you would make—you with your jealousy of everyone else, you with your interest in fame and treasure, you with your cold, cold heart. Will you really miss those other lads, do you think?"

"No," said Stefan Stinkle, and his cold heart became even colder.

"Welcome to the dragon world," said Duncan, and the smoke swirled up to hide the figure in the doorway.

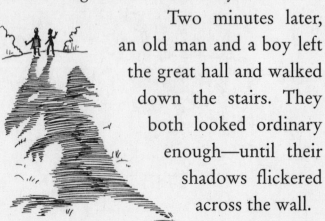

Two minutes later, an old man and a boy left the great hall and walked down the stairs. They both looked ordinary enough—until their shadows flickered across the wall.

The Dragon Slippers

Pendletwist the wizard was ambitious. He didn't want fame or fortune but he did want to be the very best wizard in the world. To stand on the podium at the annual Wizards' Convention and receive an award for A Lifetime's Achievement in Wizardry was what he really craved. In fact, he knew perfectly well that fame and

fortune might stand in his way. The award was usually given to a wizard who was respected by other wizards but had not received the recognition he deserved from the rest of the world.

Pendletwist was only interested in the judgement of his peers. He knew that ordinary people had very little idea of

what was clever in wizardry. They were impressed by what Pendletwist called "wizz-bang magic". Puffs of smoke (green for preference), loud cymbal clashes and mysterious mists pleased the unlearned much more than really difficult magic. In fact, most non-wizards didn't even realize that it is much, much more difficult to turn a seven-spot ladybird into a five-spot ladybird than it is to cure warts or find a missing key-ring. They simply had no idea of the intricacies of elegant magic.

Year after year, Pendletwist worked quietly away. Of course, he did the kinds of things that wizards usually do to make ends meet. He found cows that had strayed, sold love potions and did money-magnet magic. But most of his time was spent in perfecting new techniques for colour-change magic and writing papers about it for publication in the various learned journals read by wizards all over the world. He knew that his reputation among other wizards was high. Several of them had been known to consult him when they had a really difficult problem. As the oldest wizards of all gradually went into retirement (it's very dangerous to practise wizardry after your powers have waned) or magicked themselves off to a desert island somewhere, Pendletwist became more and more confident that he was next in line for the coveted Lifetime's Achievement in Wizardry Award. This was his year. He could feel it in his bones.

But poor old Pendletwist had not calculated on a change in the Wizardry Awards rules. Just when his turn to win was certainly coming, a Grand Gathering

of Wizards agreed that for the first time
that year witches would be eligible for the
same prizes as wizards.

Pendletwist was appalled. He hadn't
been keeping up with developments in
witchcraft and had to magic up several
years' worth of volumes of *The Witch's
Weekly* to catch up. What he read there
shocked him to the core.

Those witches were good! While the wizards had been making tiny (but important) changes in spells that had been used for centuries, the witches had broken new ground and were trying out magic that opened up possibilities the wizards had never dreamed about. They had made exciting new discoveries in the field of interplanetary travel, for example, and had set up a Cosmic Coven on Mars. They had also done a lot of work on personality improvement. Reading what they were working on, Pendletwist could think of quite a few wizards of his acquaintance who could have benefited from their attentions. It was all quite remarkable.

Although several witches were very close to Pendletwist in experience and skill, one in particular made him dread the forthcoming prize-giving. There was no doubt about it that Magda the Malevolent

was far ahead of anyone else practising magic. She had even done work on colour transformation, and her approach was both elegant and unexpected. She had gone back to some of the ancient methods, involving woad, madder and toads, and used them to devastating new effect. She was also a particularly nasty and obnoxious witch. No voter in his or her right mind would turn her down for the supreme award at this year's ceremony.

Poor old Pendletwist pondered and pondered. As far as he could see, Magda was going strong. It was unusual, of course, but he really couldn't see why she wouldn't win the supreme award for years to come. Most wizards rested on their laurels after being honoured. Pendletwist had been planning to do that himself. A cosy cave somewhere. A little light consulting work. It would be the perfect end to a very distinguished career. Somehow, he didn't think that was what Magda had in mind. She didn't seem to be the kind of witch to hang up her broomstick and take up knitting. Pendletwist saw all his dreams dissolving into dust. But what was the alternative?

For one mad moment, the wizard seriously considered trying to do away with Magda. He didn't usually delve into the black arts, but he knew the theory and didn't feel much compunction about the rapid disposal of a witch who was in his way. But a second's reflection brought Pendletwist to his senses. Taking on a witch of Magda's power was no light undertaking, and there was no guarantee that he would win, just because he had the advantage of surprise. Anyway, did he really have surprise on his side? Who knew what those witches could find out from their Cosmic Coven and Spellbinding Satellites? Pendletwist shivered. He could be being watched even now. And besides, Magda wasn't called "the Malevolent" for nothing. If he did fail to abolish her, she might take a really repulsive revenge. In fact, she would be obliged to in order not to lose face among her fellow witches (and wizards, now). Pendletwist did not allow himself to dwell for too long on the very unpleasant possibilities for perpetual pain and punishment. No, attacking Magda was far too big a risk to take.

Night after night, the poor old wizard was unable to sleep. He tossed and turned in his bed, despite taking rather more calming potions than were good for him. Then, one stormy morning, when the thunder was crashing around his home and lightning sizzled at the windows, Pendletwist suddenly saw what he must do. He must beat Magda at her own game! In short, he must make a magical discovery of such amazing power and importance that his name would live for ever in the annals of wizardry. It would be hard work. It might even be dangerous. But it would be worth it.

Pendletwist considered many areas in which he could do something stunning. It was not easy. Of course not. If it had been easy, any witch, wizard or warlock would have solved the problem years ago. As Pendletwist bent over a bubbling brew and thought long and hard, he forgot to keep a weather eye on the storm outside. Most wizards like to monitor such things. A storm is usually simply that—a storm. But just sometimes thunder and lightning are unleashed by a wizard or witch who wants to perform some dastardly magic while other magicians' minds are elsewhere. Thunder and lightning produce electrical disturbances that make wizards and witches less alert than usual. Possibly, that is what happened to Pendletwist next. We may never know.

There's no need to dwell on what befell our hero. Briefly, a bolt of lightning struck a tree near the wizard's home. This in turn fell with a mighty crash, just as Pendletwist was putting his head out of the door to catch a little rainwater for his brew. *Thwack!* A wizard's head is stronger than yours, but it isn't much of a match for a falling tree. Pendletwist was felled by the blow and lay there on his doorstep for several hours before the rain became hailstones the size of tennis balls and woke him.

As he came round, Pendletwist's brain was surprisingly clear. He knew at once what he must do. He must find a genuine pair of dragon slippers.

The idea was audacious. It had never been done before. But Pendletwist was determined and single-minded. Much can be achieved with these two qualities. There and then he began making his plans.

You have probably never heard of the dragon slippers, but perhaps you have heard of the Holy Grail, sought by King Arthur and his knights? Or you may have heard of the secret recipe that medieval alchemists searched for—one that would turn any old thing into gold. Or you may know that even as you read this, scientists are peering through their telescopes, searching the depths of space for signs of alien life. The dragon slippers were like all of these extraordinary dreams rolled into one. Wizards had tried to find them since the beginning of time (and even before that, but that's an idea that it's hard to get your head around if you're not a wizard). The dragon slippers were supposed to be guarded by a sleeping dragon of such power and ferocity that no one dared come near him—even if they could find him. He was known to be asleep in a mountain somewhere in the world, but no one knew where. To seize the slippers, a wizard would first of all have to kill the dragon—without using magic. That might not sound too difficult for a strapping knight in armour, but wizards tend to be skinny, shrivelled-looking types with the muscles of a gnat. A fight between a dragon and a wizard would be one-sided to say the least. Then, as the dragon heaves his last breath, you would have to breathe in the dying flames from his nostrils (don't try this at home!) and seize the slippers in your left hand. If you have followed all these steps exactly, you are in possession of a pair of slippers that will enable you to know everything that can be known when

you wear them on your feet. Pendletwist trembled at the thought.

We need not follow in detail the tedious months during which the wizard perfected his dragon-detector. His first effort was very effective, but the machine was too large to go through the door. It took Pendletwist a long time to develop a pocket-sized detector. Then, packing his wizard's bag and throwing on his most magical cloak, Pendletwist set off on his extraordinary quest.

Once again, we will skip over the trudging and tramping that took the weary wizard from one end of the world to the other. Suffice it to say that one day he came to a mountain that looked a good

deal more menacing than any he had yet encountered on his travels. And the dial of his dragon-detector was spinning madly. Pendletwist felt a cold fear around his knees as he looked up at the mountain and realized that the dragon lay within.

Never has a wizard crept on quieter feet than Pendletwist when he slunk into a gaping cavern in the side of the mountain. A winding passageway led down and down and down, right into the heart of the rock, and as it wound, the air became hotter, until it was hard for the wizard to breathe. At last, in a cavern lit by an eerie glow, he found the sleeping dragon. Its scales gleamed in the light of the flames that flickered from its nose. Its breathing was like a hot, rushing wind, flattening poor Pendletwist against the wall of the cave. Paralysed with fear, he clung to the rock, unable to decide what to do next.

Sometimes, just sometimes, fate takes as big a hand in the affairs of wizards as it does in the affairs of humankind. The terrified wizard was clutching the only piece of rock in the entire cave that was *loose*. As Pendletwist's knees trembled, he leaned a little more of his weight on the rock, and the rock, followed by half of the wall of the cave, came crashing down, missing the wizard by millimetres but thudding with unerring accuracy on to the head of the sleeping dragon. The dragon's eyes flickered open for an instant and then it was no more. A great rasping sound filled Pendletwist's ears as the dragon breathed its last fiery breath.

He was almost too late. Out of the corner of his eye, Pendletwist spied the dragon slippers. Seizing them with his left hand, he leapt forward to breath in the last flickering flames from the dragon's huge nostrils. It was like the nastiest medicine you've ever tasted. It was like the foulest smell you've ever smelt. It was horrible beyond belief. And then it was over.

Pendletwist couldn't believe his luck. He stood there, shaking in his shoes and clasping the slippers to his skinny chest. Somehow, he had done it. He had found the dream of every wizard. He would be famous for ever more. And best of all, he would undoubtedly receive the Lifetime's Achievement Award at the next Joint Wizards and Witches Convention.

Pendletwist staggered out of the cave and into the fresh air. He had no idea how to find his way home, but he knew that all his problems would be solved as soon as he put on the slippers. They were beautiful slippers and, from time to time, little puffs of smoke and flame came from their heels. They were clearly raring to go. As soon as he wore them, Pendletwist would know all that there was to know— including the fastest way home. He sat down and kicked off his wizard's boots. Gingerly, he inserted one toe into a smoking dragon slipper.

"Problems, Pendletwist?" cackled an amused voice behind him.

The wizard knew in one instant two quite unconnected but equally terrible things. Firstly, the dragon slippers were much, much too small for him. They would never, ever fit on his feet. Secondly,

the voice that rang unpleasantly in his ears and made his nerves jangle could only belong to one person.

"I take it that I am addressing Magda the Malevolent?" he said wearily.

"Well done, Pendletwist," laughed Magda. "You've saved me a lot of work. Fiddling about with dragon-detectors was never my idea of fun. Those slippers, on the other hand, are *just* what I need."

Pendletwist didn't see any point in arguing. He had been beaten from the start. He knew in his bones that Magda's small, fat feet would fit those dragon slippers perfectly. He was right.

You don't need to ask who won the Lifetime's Achievement Award that year—and every year since. Pendletwist, to be fair, did go down in history as the finder of the slippers. He became famous and made his fortune appearing on chat shows. Which just goes to show that very often in life you get just what you didn't want—unless you're Magda the Malevolent, of course.

The Dreaming Dragon

Dragons in stories spend a lot of time rampaging about the countryside, eating young maidens and being killed by handsome knights. If they're not doing that, they are lurking in their caves, guarding their fabulous treasure. Of course, it is true that dragons do all those things— some of the time. But most of the time they are not rampaging, breathing their last or guarding—they are simply sleeping.

It's not that dragons are lazy. It's not that they hibernate in cold weather, either. It's simply that breathing fire takes an enormous amount of energy. Dragons have developed a way of conserving their energy (you may find your father or grandfather uses a similar technique). They simply sleep as often and as deeply as they possibly can.

It is, in fact, the sleeping, rather than the need to hide their treasure, that causes dragons to prefer living in caves. Dragons have a reputation for being ferocious and dangerous. It's a reputation which, for obvious reasons, they are keen to keep up. A sleeping dragon is, frankly, a pretty easy target, especially if you don't mind getting your sleeves singed. Dragons need a safe place to sleep, well away from young and ambitious knights with reputations of their own to build.

Every so often, a dragon decides that he or she is fed up with living in a cave and looks for an alternative. But dragons are large creatures. They can't hide under a rock or squiggle down a burrow. One or two of them have tried taking to the water, but in doing so they lose the name of dragon and have to be called sea serpents. You see, they simply can't breathe fire underwater. It doesn't work.

Other dragons have opted for deep, dark forests to hide in. That, on the face of it, isn't a bad solution. Sadly, breathing fire is even more of a problem when you are surrounded by wood. You will, I am sure, have read about the terrible forest fires experienced in some countries. They are often blamed on careless campers or pipe-smoking ramblers. The real culprits are a little larger than either of those innocent parties. Need I say more?

Wise dragons know that when you are looking for a home, you can't beat a good cave—the larger and drier the better. It should have plenty of room for treasure and give the dragon room to stretch and wriggle a little in his or her sleep. A cave that's a little too small can be unbelievably uncomfortable.

Dragons, like many reptiles, keep growing all their lives. That is why some of them reach such an extraordinary size. As a rule of thumb, a large dragon is an old dragon. And an old dragon is a wily dragon. Smaller, younger dragons may be quicker on their feet, but they can also be pretty stupid.

The dragon in this story was still a youngster when he found his own perfect cave. Like most youngsters, he was looked after by his mother until he could fend for himself. All mother dragons teach their children the time-honoured techniques of village-scaring, maiden-munching, knight-frying and treasure-hunting. When they have a good basic understanding of these important matters, it is time for young dragons to go out into the world and find caves of their own. It is usually springtime when they trot off on their own, which is why early spring is not a very good time of the year to wander about alone among the mountains. Young dragons are notorious for starting avalanches by a bit of careless breathing.

It was, indeed, a very fine spring day when our dragon, whose name was Arvul, set off into the big wide world. He trotted along happily enough, frightening any sheep he came across for practice. He was on the lookout for a large, dry cave, just as his mother had taught him.

It's never easy finding a new home. Arvul poked his nose into one or two holes in the mountainside that had the audacity to *call* themselves caves but really weren't large enough to house a griffin, never mind a dragon. He also wandered into another couple that were distinctly damp. He could tell that by the way his breath sizzled when it licked the walls. No dragon wants to sleep in a damp cave. If your treasure is good quality—gold, silver and jewels—it will not come to very much harm, but there is always the danger that your flames will go out. Once out, it is an incredibly difficult business to get a dragon's flames going again.

After two days of fruitless searching, Arvul came to a very pretty valley. Three villages nestled in its hollows, and it was surrounded by imposing mountains that looked like very desirable residences.

Arvul looked about with pleasure. He was already beginning to feel very tired after his walk. What he needed, he knew, was a few years' sleep. At one end of the valley, there was a large castle, standing on its own small hill a little above one of the villages. Above the castle, high up on the

mountainside, Arvul found what he thought was the perfect cave. Of course, after seeing some less-than-perfect caves, his standards had dropped a little. The cave was not as spacious as he would have liked, but it would do. Arvul eyed the setting sun and decided that there was just time to visit the castle, snack on a maiden or two, and pick up a little treasure to make the place feel like home.

He was in luck. Most of the knights of the castle were off fighting a battle somewhere, and the castle was practically undefended. Arvul flew down into the courtyard with a few fearsome squawks.

The reaction to Arvul's arrival was very gratifying. Servants ran up and down without a clue what to do. All castles keep some basic equipment for dealing with dragons, but it is only as good as the people using it. In this case, the chief steward hadn't bothered to hold a dragon practice for years, so the fire-quenching buckets were empty and the tail-prodder could not be found. Arvul had all the time in the world to do whatever he liked.

In other respects, the castle was a little disappointing. There were very few maidens to be found, so Arvul had to make do with a rather bony cook and a couple of goats. Treasure was a little thin on the ground, too. But he did manage to find a couple of coronets and two small bags of gold coins. It wasn't much, but it was a start. Arvul flew back to his new home, well pleased with his first day as a homeowner. He put the treasure carefully in a corner of his cave and settled down to go to sleep.

The influence of dragon dreams on the human population of the world has been very little studied. Folk tales tell, of course, that an unhappy dragon living near a village brings bad weather, sour milk, ugly babies and terribly boring storytellers. This is usually put down to the strain that the villagers are under, wondering each day when the dragon will wake up and come rampaging. As a matter of fact, that isn't what causes the problems at all. The dragon is having unpleasant dreams, which affect everything going on

around him. If he has tummy trouble, for example, as can happen if he swallows a maiden wearing a suit of armour or even a lot of jewellery, his dreams are likely to be dark and spiky. Thunder, hailstones as big as footballs, and rivers overflowing their banks are likely to be the result. On the other hand, if you have a dragon living nearby who has sweet dreams, things can be truly wonderful. Flowers will bloom, crops will grow, little lambs will gambol in the fields, and all will be well.

That is exactly how it was for the first couple of years that Arvul lived above the pleasant valley. Although news of the attack on the castle had frightened the people there badly, it is hard to be really terrified when the sun is shining and little birds are singing from the blossoming branches. In a few months, the memory of the dragon's visit faded away and any number of idyllic country pursuits were carried on—dancing on the green, singing around the village pump, garlanding anything that moved with flowers—you know the kind of thing.

It was only very, very gradually that things began to change. The weather grew a little worse each year. Winter lasted longer and summer seemed briefer. A nasty little green caterpillar attacked all the cabbages. An even nastier disease crept on to the roses around the cottage doors. It happened so gradually that no one noticed for a very long time. And certainly no one understood why.

You, with your superior knowledge of dragon lore, have probably guessed already. It was, of course, because Arvul, up in his cave in the mountainside, was having very bad dreams. The reason for this is more interesting, and a warning to young dragons everywhere. You see, Arvul was growing. He was a young dragon, so he was growing quite quickly. The cave, however, wasn't. Growing, that is. Year by year, Arvul was more and more cramped in his mountainside home. His breath scorched the walls. His claws bit into the rock. He bumped his head every time he tried to turn over (and another couple of stones tumbled off the castle walls and into the moat below).

An older dragon, feeling his back rubbing against the rock and his chin being pierced by a coronet, would probably wake up and try to put things right. But although he was growing, Arvul was still a young dragon. He slept, as he did almost everything else, wholeheartedly. For another couple of years, he slept. He became more and more uncomfortable. His dreams became worse and worse. Down in the valley, the steeple fell off the church and the chickens stopped laying. Some black, slimy stuff started oozing out of the river and a couple of wolves had a party in the sheep-pen at least once a week.

It was just then that two remarkable things happened at exactly the same time. The knights from the castle, having finished their battle at last, came home, bringing with them a wizard they had found in a dungeon. At the same moment, Arvul woke up and found himself not only deeply uncomfortable but stuck! He was too large now to get through the narrow entrance to the cave.

Now, for the first time, the knights heard about the dragon's visit all those years before. It annoyed them. Knights who come home from a battle, especially a long battle, have lots of stories to tell. They are looking for a willing audience and a good deal of "Oh, how brave you were! How terrible it must have been for you!" What they do not want is to find that someone else is expecting to hear the same thing in return.

One young knight, however, who had been little more than a boy when he had left to win his spurs, felt upset for a different reason. The bony cook, munched up by the dragon for want of any tasty maidens, had been this knight's aunt. He had also been very fond of her cooking. It seemed to him outrageous that a dragon should deprive him of the plum puddings he had been dreaming of all the time he had been away. Something, he decided, had to be done.

At this point, the young knight did something very sensible indeed. He went to consult the captured wizard. He knew that wizards very often know a great deal about dragons and can often point you in the right direction if you are trying to find one. The wizard, who was by no means stupid, saw a way to regain his freedom. He agreed at once to direct the knight to the dragon's lair on one small and simple condition.

"I will need to come with you," he said. "A cornered dragon is particularly vicious. You may need my help."

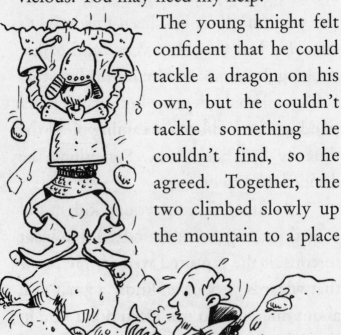

The young knight felt confident that he could tackle a dragon on his own, but he couldn't tackle something he couldn't find, so he agreed. Together, the two climbed slowly up the mountain to a place where the cunning wizard had spotted a few pathetic plumes of smoke rising from the craggy rocks.

It was a pitiful sight that met their eyes. Peering through the too-small entrance to the cave, Arvul really did not look very fearsome. The young knight drew his sword at once. But as he approached the doorway, he felt a little uneasy. It was one thing to kill a dragon in a terrific battle. Maidens would be falling over themselves to get to him for the rest of his life. But to kill a dragon who could not escape, who was powerless and looking up at him with big, bright eyes, did not seem to be the act of a gentleman. The knight paused and looked enquiringly at the wizard.

The wizard, interested only in his own future, could see the difficulty. He could also see Arvul's small pile of treasure, squashed to one side of the cave.

"Let's not do anything too hasty," he said. He didn't fancy having to hack through heaps of dead dragon to reach the coronets and gold coins.

The wizard wandered out of the cave and stomped about a bit on the mountainside. The knight sat down at the entrance to the cave and guarded the dragon—not that poor Arvul was going anywhere at all.

At last the wizard returned. He was breathless and looked excited.

"I've found another entrance!" he said. "It's larger than this one and leads out of a much bigger cave, but it's blocked up with rocks. We could move them and get to the tr... dragon."

The wizard wasn't used to much physical work, but the young knight was keen to exercise his muscles. He moved five rocks for every one that the wizard, wheezing and wingeing, managed to shift. It was a long job, but at last...

"Be careful, now," the wizard said. "This is the last one. The dragon may make a run for it."

The last rock was flung aside, and the knight and the wizard leapt back out of the way. In rushed Arvul, stretching his wings in joy in the larger cave. The wizard hid behind a rock. The knight readied himself for a mighty battle. Arvul curled up happily and went right back to sleep.

The poor young knight stood there with his mouth open. He wished now that he had killed the dragon when he was trapped. He certainly didn't feel that it was a knightly thing to kill a dragon when he was asleep. He was still wondering what to do when the wizard, appearing at his elbow, gave him some very good advice. Which just shows how well a wizard can think with a couple of bags of treasure tucked into his robe.

"My advice," he said, "would be to leave him here. I think you'll find that things have improved a great deal down in the valley. And everyone will think you are a great hero when you bring these two coronets back."

The knight felt an enormous sense of relief and sheathed his sword. The wizard felt an enormous sense of wealth and silently slipped away. Arvul felt an even more enormous sense of comfort. He stirred happily in his sleep as his dreams became filled with all the things that a dragon likes best: treasure, and maidens, and warm, dry caves, and mothers, and maidens, and treasure.

The knight looked for the wizard for a while, but he was not really sorry to see him go. It had occurred to him that without witnesses of what had happened on the mountain, he might well be able to embroider his encounter with the dragon a little. There was no need to tell anyone that the dragon was sleeping peacefully.

Down in the valley, the knight could hardly recognize the village he had left. Blossoms dangled, birds chirruped and villagers sang. Every so often, a gentle shower sprinkled the fields with a light dusting of diamonds, and the river sparkled once more.

The Dragon Tamer

Once upon a time, in a country far away, there was a town with a very serious dragon problem. For centuries, a dragon had lived in the mountains a few miles from the town. Every few years, she came into town and set fire to a few roofs, ate a few cows, and stole anything glittery that caught her eye. It was a nuisance, of course, but it wasn't a huge problem. The town fire brigade got very good at putting out roof-fires. The townsfolk got very good at hiding their valuables. And the cows got very good at running. It didn't do them any good, I'm afraid, as dragons can run faster, but they looked very fit and healthy—for cows.

The visits of the dragon, as I said, were annoying but not serious. Then, one year, things suddenly got a good deal worse. This time when the dragon visited, she set fire to the town hall and the church, stole the entire contents of the bank vaults, and ate three grandmothers and a great-uncle. It was a disaster.

When they had recovered from the shock, the townsfolk got together to decide what should be done.

"I don't understand it!" cried the Mayor. "I've lost as many cows as the next man in the past, but when it comes to my dear old granny, that's another thing! This can't go on!"

The Minister was inclined to take a hopeful view.

"Maybe it won't—go on, I mean," he said. "For all we know, this is a one-off incident, caused by the phase of the moon or the weather or something. We've never had real trouble from that dragon before. In fact, I've always felt that having a dragon near the town made us rather distinguished. This unfortunate—you do have my sympathies, Mr. Mayor, as do all those who have been bereaved—incident will, I trust, never be repeated."

Many of the townsfolk wanted to believe this. In the end, the Mayor was shouted down and it was agreed to do nothing at all. After all, there were usually at least five or seven years between the visits of the dragon. They had plenty of time to think of a plan if it was decided that action must be taken after all.

The townspeople went back to their homes and tried to forget all about the dragon. The bank vaults were reinforced. The town hall and the church were repaired. The grandmothers and the great-uncle were mourned. Life went on as usual—for a couple of months.

Only eight weeks after the dragon's fatal visit, the town awoke one morning to find that she had been again. Already! A scene of devastation met the eyes of all those who woke up on that fateful morning—and that wasn't as many as there should have been by a long chalk.

The jeweller's shop had been raided and the entire stock removed. Two whole streets had been burned to the ground. And worst of all, over twenty men, women and children were unaccounted for. At first, it was hoped that some of them had died in the fires. That seems a strange thing to hope, but the alternative was much, much worse. When not a trace of a body was found in the ashes, the people of the town had to face an unpleasant fact. The dragon was getting hungrier and didn't seem to mind *what* or *who* she ate.

For a few days, the townsfolk were so shocked that they could do nothing. Then, gradually, they each began to cope with the situation in different ways. A group of young lads formed the Town Dragon Defence League and held regular training sessions in the square. The Minister set up a Dragon Awareness Seminar for all

those who wanted to confront their fears.
The jeweller and several other families

packed up all their belongings and set off
to find somewhere else to live. Once
again, a few people simply tried not to
think about it.

The dragon's third visit within four
months happened only six weeks later.
She attacked in daylight—an unheard of
event—and rampaged up and down the
main street, roaring and lashing her tail to

left and right. It was a terrifying sight. She ate the Minister and twelve members of his congregation. Their Dragon Awareness was no help at all. The Town Dragon Defence League, gallantly trying to defend their nearest and dearest, suffered a similar fate. Worst of all, the dragon sat down in the town square and wouldn't move for over six hours. The townspeople crouched in their homes, terrified. Was she planning to stay there for ever?

At last, as dusk fell, the dragon headed back to the mountains. As she flew over the roof-tops, she snarled and shook her head from side to side, scorching the trees beneath.

In the town the next morning, white, shocked faces lined the square when the Mayor called a Council of War.

"I will be frank with you, good people," he said, "I don't know what to do."

A shudder of fear ran through the crowd at the Mayor's admission. They felt alone and lost, at the mercy of a fearful force they did not understand. Then, at the back of the crowd, a girl stood up.

"Your Worship," she called, "I don't know if this is any help. It's just, well, that sometimes an expert can think of things that we can't."

An expert? A murmer ran through the crowd as the girl passed a folded piece of paper to the front. When it reached the Mayor, he looked at it in silence. He pursed his lips doubtfully, but really, what option did he have?

"I will read you what this says," said the Mayor, raising his voice to address the whole crowd. "It is an advertisement. It says: 'Do you have a dragon problem? Call on Eldwing Plooc, Dragon Tamer. Many recommendations available from satisfied customers. Mad bulls also a speciality.'"

"Call him! Call him now!" called the crowd. "Anything is better than sitting here and waiting to be eaten!"

There was an address on the piece of paper, but the Mayor decided not to rely on the rather erratic postal service. He called his own son to deliver the message in person. The sooner this Dragon Tamer arrived, the better. And Norridge was a sensible boy. He could be relied upon.

The Mayor calculated that it would take Norridge a week to find the Dragon Tamer and bring him back again. It was the longest week of his life. On the sixth day, the Mayor had a sudden thought that perhaps the Dragon Tamer would not be at home when Norridge came knocking. He might be out at the other end of the kingdom, taming another dragon.

But the Mayor need not have worried. Exactly one week after Norridge had set out on his best white pony, two figures were seen riding towards the town. As they drew nearer, it could be seen that the man riding alongside the Mayor's son was seated on a jet black horse with multi-coloured plumes on its head. To a town in mourning, those plumes looked unnecessarily festive. Was this man really what he claimed?

Norridge and the Dragon Tamer rode into the main square. He was a tall, thin creature, with strange clothes of many different colours.

"He looks as if he belongs in a circus," said the Mayor to his wife. "I hope I haven't made a dreadful mistake. These people deserve better than a charlatan."

At the town well, the Dragon Tamer turned to greet the Mayor. That gentleman found himself looking into the deepest, darkest eyes he had ever seen. He felt very uncomfortable. It was as though the odd stranger could read his mind.

"Yes," said the man, "I am Eldwing Plooc, Dragon Tamer. And no, I can't read your mind."

"Oh, good," said the Mayor with relief, before realizing that this answer to an unasked question was even more worrying.

"No doubt my son has told you of our trouble," he said. "Can you help us?"

"That depends," said Eldwing Plooc. "Can you help me?"

"You mean payment?" asked the Mayor, more and more convinced that he was talking to a confidence trickster. "I'm sure we can come to a fair arrangement. We were thinking of something in the region of six hundred florins."

The crowd gasped. Six hundred florins was an enormous amount of money. But the Dragon Tamer laughed.

"Is that all?" he grinned. "Why, the dragon took more than that on her first visit. Surely you can do better than that?"

The Mayor looked again into the dark, disturbing eyes.

"I have an idea," he said. "If you can deal with the dragon, you can have half the treasure that she took from us. How about that? It will come to a very great deal of money. You will be set up for life."

But the Dragon Tamer shook his head vigorously.

"Oh no," he said. "I couldn't do that. It wouldn't be fair to the dragon. I can only deal with her on an open and honest basis. If I went around stealing from my clients, word would soon get around. No, that treasure belongs to the dragon now. You will never see it again."

The Mayor was stunned.

"I think there is a misunderstanding here," he said coldly. "*We* are your clients, not the dragon. You are working for us. We would be happy to see the dragon killed. Indeed, we assumed that "taming" was a polite way of talking about just that."

"Did you?" asked Eldwing. "Then I'm afraid you are wrong. Eldwing Plooc only ever works for the strongest party in a case. In this instance, I believe that is the dragon. And although technically *you* have called me in, it is really the dragon's cry for help that I am answering."

"Cry for help?" The Mayor couldn't believe his ears. "She's a *dragon*, for goodness sake. Dragons do this kind of thing! We don't need to waste time feeling sorry for a creature that has burned our homes and killed our families. Maybe she doesn't know any better, but that's neither here nor there.

The dragon has to go, and we have called you to make sure that she never troubles us again. I don't care how you do it. Just get it over with as quickly as possible!"

The Dragon Tamer remained as impassive as a stone. He talked to the Mayor as if he was a small boy with a muddy face.

"Let me explain something," he said. "Dragons are gentle creatures on the whole. They spend their days sleeping. They may eat the odd cow. They may take the odd trinket. But other than that and a very little involuntary arson, they do no harm. Didn't your dragon use to be like that?"

"Well, yes," admitted the Mayor. "But surely that's not the point. The dragon has gone mad and needs to be stopped."

"You miss my meaning," replied Eldwing Plooc. "Dragons do not attack unless they are provoked in some way. What did you do to the dragon?"

"Do to the dragon? Nothing! We never touched the dragon!"

"Forgive me, but that cannot be true," insisted the stranger. "Did someone swipe at her with a sword?"

"No! No!" The Mayor was almost ashamed to say it.

"A spear was thrown, perhaps?"

"No! Nothing like that at all!"

"Cows were poisoned?"

"Of course not! We never knew when the dragon was going to attack. We wouldn't have any cows left if we kept poisoning them. We're careful to look after our cows."

The Dragon Tamer stroked his chin.

"Indeed? In what way?"

"I don't see what this has to do..." began the Mayor, but something in the stranger's face stopped him. "If we're going to go into detail about animal husbandry, you'd better come into the town hall and sit down," he said. "I'll call my stockman to talk to you as well."

For the next two hours, the stranger heard everything there was to hear about the fine animals kept by the Mayor and other townspeople. He asked questions about everything—their feed, their bedding, their milking and their calving.

"It sounds to me as if you have a very busy life," he told the stockman. "Only at night do you have a chance to sit down by your own fireside."

"Oh, well, and even then there are the cow-bells to polish," laughed the stockman.

The Dragon Tamer stiffened. "Cow-bells? Why do you have those?" he asked with a curious glint in his eye.

"So that the cows don't stray, of course," said the stockman. "One or two of them used to wander off towards the mountains. And what with the dragon and all... We thought bells would help us to find them if they wandered."

"And when," asked the stranger, rising to his feet, "were these bells introduced? There's no need to answer. I can tell *you*. It was sometime before the dragon's first vicious attack and after her last "normal" visit. Am I right?"

The Mayor and the stockman nodded their heads. For the life of them, they could not see the significance of the cow-bells.

"Now," said Eldwing Plooc briskly, "I think we can solve this little matter very quickly. Please take me to your doctor."

Eldwing Plooc was closeted with the doctor for fifteen minutes. He came back into the square carrying a large medical case, which he strapped to his horse. Then, without another word, he leapt into the saddle and set off towards the mountains.

"Well?" said the Mayor, clutching the doctor's sleeve in his agitation. "What did he talk about? What did he want? Will we ever see him again?"

"I certainly hope so," said the doctor. "I don't like it, but he was very persuasive. Something about those eyes... He has taken my whole stock of sleeping drugs. You can understand why I'm worried. In the wrong hands..."

"I'll give him twenty-four hours," said the Mayor. "Then I'm reporting him to the authorities as a fraudster. Meanwhile, what am I going to tell the people? They'll lose confidence in me, I'm sure."

The Mayor need not have worried. The next morning, at about ten o'clock, an extraordinary sight met his eyes as he came out into the square. There was Eldwing Plooc, walking large as life into the town, and with him, following as meekly as a lamb, was the dragon!

"It was simple, when I heard about the cow-bells," explained the Dragon Tamer. "I realized at once that the dragon had broken her teeth on those sharp metal objects. The pain drove her almost mad. You really cannot blame her. With help from the doctor's medicine chest, I have repaired the damage. She (and her name is Ebelu, by the way, it would be more polite if you would use it) has come to make amends by helping out your blacksmith for a few days. All will be well. Now, about my fee…"

Settling the fee took a good deal longer than solving the problem, but the town returned to normal at last. Today, you would never know about its time of trouble, except that every inhabitant—but none of the cows—wears a cow-bell around his or her neck. It seems a sensible precaution!

The Dragon on the Carpet

Wizards live to a very great age, but the time comes when even they have to say their last spell and hang up their wands. When Russell's ancient great-grandfather closed his eyes for the last time, several members of the family nodded their heads mysteriously and said, "About time too!"

"That's not very nice, is it?" Russell asked his mother, who was gardening. "I mean, no one *wanted* him to die, did they? Or was he really old and ill? I wish I'd met him just once."

"He lived a long way away," said his mother, putting down her secateurs, "and no, of course no one *wanted* him to die. He was in incredibly good health and quite disgustingly energetic. It's just that it was a bit embarrassing having him still around, if you see what I mean."

"Well, no, I don't," said Russell. "How could he be embarrassing if you never saw him?"

Mrs. Miravelo looked at her son thoughtfully. She wondered if he was old enough to be told. Well, she had been much the same age...

"It was his age that was getting embarrassing," she said, "explaining it, I mean. People were starting to ask awkward questions. It's so much more difficult these days with birth certificates and so on. Centuries ago, there was so little paperwork that it was simple."

Russell had no idea what she was talking about.

"*What* was embarrassing about his age?" he asked. "How old was he?"

Mrs. Miravelo gulped. "Three hundred and forty-nine," she said.

Russell laughed. And stopped. His mother wasn't laughing. She was kind of wincing at the thought of explaining something tricky.

"Perhaps we'd better go in and get some cold drinks or something," she said. "Then I can tell you properly."

Russell and his mother sat under a tree with cans of drink and a bag of crisps. His mother seemed to be eating rather a lot of them. Russell fixed her with his fiercest look and said, "Tell me!"

"He really was three hundred and forty-nine," she said. "He liked to pretend he was only three hundred and twelve, but it wasn't true. He was born the same year as your great-great-great-great-great-great-great-great-great-great-great-great-great grandmother on the other side, so I always remember."

Russell took another swig of his drink. His mother had been in the sun too long. How could his great-grandfather possibly be as old as that? And how could his mother remember all those other greats? It was ridiculous. But when he looked at her face, he could tell she wasn't ill or joking. She just looked a bit worried.

"Maybe I should have told you before," she said. "It just never seemed the right moment. And your father, of course, wasn't very keen for me to tell you at all."

"Tell me what?" asked Russell. A dozen ideas ran through his head. Was he adopted? Were they on the run from the police? Was his great-grandfather mad? Did it run in the family? None of these ideas were as weird as what his mother said next.

"He was a wizard, you see," she said. "I couldn't take you to see him when you were small enough to tell all your friends about it. He wasn't very good at hiding it. He came from a time when you could be burnt at the stake for being a wizard, so when they stopped burning people, he stopped being so careful. I know that the first thing he would have done would have been to magic some flowers out of your ear or turn the car into a pumpkin."

"Oh," said Russell, seeing the light at last. "You don't mean he was a wizard. You mean he was a conjuror."

"No, I don't. Conjurors don't live to three hundred and forty-nine. I mean he was a wizard. A conjuror is someone who can do tricks. Your great-grandfather didn't do tricks. He did magic. It's a different thing altogether."

"But wizards don't really exist, do they?" asked Russell. He couldn't quite believe he was having this conversation.

"They certainly do," said his mother. "You're talking to one. I don't practise, of course. I never really wanted to do all the training involved, so I'm afraid I failed my Wizard Class I paper. I sort of did it on purpose. I didn't really want to be different from everyone else. Now I rather regret it. But it's too late for me. I could never catch up now. Your grandparents were furious with me at the time, but they don't seem as bothered about it now."

Russell's thoughts were whirling, but only that came spinning to the surface in a recognizable form.

"You can't be a wizard," he said. "You'd have to be a witch."

Mrs. Miravelo sat up a little straighter. "It is a total fallacy," she said, "put about by people who don't have the first idea about magic, that women can't be wizards. Just ask your grandmother. My mother, that is, not your father's."

"Why not his?" asked Russell.

"Well, she's not a wizard. She's just human," explained his mother. "It's only my side of the family that can do magic."

Another question bubbled to the top of Russell's brain. It was a pretty important one.

"So I take after Dad, then?" he said.

"Do you?" Mrs. Miravelo looked at her son sharply. "Don't you know?"

"Well, I can't do magic," said Russell. "I've never had any weird experiences or done something I couldn't explain. I don't think you've passed it on to me. Maybe I'd have to be a seventh son or something."

"Oh, that's all nonsense!" cried Mrs. Miravelo briskly. "Well, if you think you're not, then you're not. It's a pity in a way, but it will save you a lot of trouble in the end. And I was dreading having to help you with your wizardry homework. I'm so rusty, it's embarrassing."

Over the next few days, Russell thought a lot about what his mother had said. It explained many things that had puzzled him, such as why his relatives on his mother's side were all so strange. And how his cousin Marla had been able to jump off the roof last summer without hurting herself. For a brief moment, he wished that he could have magical powers, too. Then he felt relieved again that he hadn't. It was bad enough having ordinary homework, without that wizardry stuff on top.

Russell went with his parents to his great-grandfather's funeral. He had never been to a funeral before, but he had seen them on television. He suspected that little puffs of green smoke were not supposed to come out of the coffin, and some of the other people present looked pretty odd. Russell stayed near the back with his father, as his mother went up to throw a flower in the grave at the end.

"She's been practising all week," said his father glumly. "I hope she gets it right or we'll never hear the last of it. I've no idea why they asked her to do it. They all know she doesn't do magic these days."

Some of his father's dread percolated through to Russell. What was she going to *do*? Russell hoped with all his might that it wasn't something embarrassing.

But it was something very sweet. As she neared the graveside, Mrs. Miravelo

took a quick look to see that the Minister had his back turned and threw her white lily into the grave. As it fell from her hand, she said, "Arv*lah*!" (or something very similar), and the flower turned into a white dove, which fluttered up, up, up into the sky until it was lost from view. Several old ladies nearby sighed and wiped their eyes.

"Beautifully done," said one, patting Russell on the shoulder. "You must be very proud of your dear mother."

Proud wasn't exactly the word, Russell thought. But he *was* pretty impressed. It's not everyone's mother who can do that kind of thing.

On the way home in the car, Russell asked lots of questions. His mother seemed a lot more relaxed, now that she had done her bit.

"Were they all wizards, the people who were there?" he asked. "I suppose that old lady in the purple cloak was."

"Good gracious, no, that was just great-grandfather's chiropodist," laughed Mrs. Miravelo. "Lots of the others *were* wizards, though. It was a great honour that Jupitus came."

"Jupitus? Who's he?"

"He's a very, very powerful wizard, probably the greatest in the world today. He very rarely appears in public. It just shows how famous great-grandfather was in his day."

"Was Jupitus the tall, distinguished man with the grey hair?"

"No, he's a little, short man, and he's bald. You really must stop trying to judge people by appearances, Russell. It's what's on the inside of a wizard that counts. If it comes to that, it's what's on the inside of any person that counts." She put her hand on her husband's arm and smiled at him.

"I don't know whether to be flattered or insulted," he smiled. "As you know, I haven't always seen eye to eye with your family over the years, but I thought they put on a good show today. And you were brilliant! It reminded me of our wedding."

"I did doves then," Russell's mother told him. "Only it went a bit wrong. I was trying to get them to come out in pastel colours, to match the bridesmaids' dresses, but I got confused in all the excitement. They were white but they scattered multi-coloured … er … messages all over the congregation."

Mr. Miravelo roared with laughter.

"It was priceless!" he said. "Luckily everyone thought it was some sort of liquid confetti. It was a nice idea, though."

"Don't," said Russell with emphasis, "ever think of doing anything like that at one of my parties. I am not having my friends covered with poo for *any* reason. What would I tell them? 'Oh, sorry, my mother's a wizard but she didn't do enough homework'?"

"I made a solemn vow after my wedding never to do magic again unless I was asked to," said Mrs. Miravelo, "which is why I was so pleased it went well today. I hadn't done anything for years."

It was a few weeks later, when great-grandfather's estate had been sorted out, that a delivery van drew up at the family's front door.

"A delivery for a Mr. R. Miravelo," said the driver. "Is this the right house?"

"That will be my son," said Russell's mother. "I'll sign for it."

When Russell came home, she told him that a very large package was waiting for him in the hall.

"It was left to you by your great-grandfather," she said. "I don't know what made him think of you. I expect he left something to all his great-grandchildren. I wouldn't get too excited, if I were you. I don't think he had anything valuable."

The package took ages to undo. At first sight what it contained wasn't very exciting. It was a large piece of carpet, with tassels at the edges and a big picture of a

dragon woven into the middle of it. It was rather worn and tatty.

"I'm sorry, sweetheart," said Russell's mother. "It's not very interesting, is it? Shall I take it down to the charity shop?"

Russell shook his head.

"No, I'll have it in my room for a while, before I decide what to do. After all, not everyone has a wizard's carpet."

The carpet fitted perfectly. From his bed, Russell could see the curvy shape of the dragon. A wizard's carpet! Russell climbed out of bed and sat down in the middle of the dragon. For the first time, he thought about his great-grandfather and what it would have meant to be a wizard. He wondered if his mother was, in spite of what she had said, disappointed not to have a wizard son. On the other hand, she had married his father, so she must quite like non-wizards.

Russell shut his eyes. If only it was a magic carpet that could carry him all over the world. How wonderful that would be! Russell almost felt as if he was floating. Surely it felt as if the carpet was shifting slightly beneath him? But when he opened his eyes, he was firmly on the floor again. He felt rather childish for wishing such a thing. But knowing what he knew now, he could no longer harbour thoughts of magic as suitable only for babies and tiny children. He thought again of what his mother had done at the funeral. His father had been proud. Now he realized that he was, too. He was proud to come from a long line of wizards. He was sorry that the line ended with his mother. For the first time, he felt a little sad that he wasn't magical himself.

How did people know that they had magical powers? How had cousin Marla known that she could jump off a roof and not hurt herself? Was it just confidence? No, that would be hopeless. She must  know somehow, deep inside. All of a sudden, Russell felt that he needed to know for sure. He hurried to the telephone.

When his cousin heard what he wanted to know, she laughed.

"No, I didn't feel anything special. I just always knew," she said. "But then I always knew there were wizards in the family, so I kind of assumed I would be one, too. It didn't  occur to me that I might not be. What makes you think that you're not one?"

"The fact that nothing makes me think that I am one," said Russell. "I'd know by now, wouldn't I? I mean, nothing weird has ever happened to me—except having a mother who's a wizard."

"Well, have you ever tried?" asked Marla. "Of course nothing will happen if you don't try. Just have a go at something simple. Anything will do. I've got to go now. Let me know how you get on!"

Russell walked back into his room. He felt ridiculous. Try what? Try how? He looked at the dragon on the carpet and spoke out loud.

"All right," he said, "let's see you turn yourself into a *real* dragon."

The dragon on the carpet stretched and yawned, but Russell was already half-way down the stairs.

"Mum!" he cried, bursting into the kitchen. "I think I need help with my wizardry homework, and I need it *now*!"

"What…?" began his mother.

Then she, too, heard the squelch of dragon feet coming down the stairs.

The Fearless, Fireless Dragon

I don't know if you have ever thought about the extraordinary way in which dragons breathe fire. Everyone knows they do it, but scientists have never been able to get close enough to one to find out exactly how it works. For one thing, why don't dragons singe their own nostrils? The firefighting forces of the world would dearly like to find out. It could save them a fortune on fire-proof suits.

Another good question that is often asked concerns baby dragons. As you know, dragons hatch from eggs—big eggs. Like most babies, they don't actually start breathing until they are out in the world. In any case, breathing fire *inside* an egg is asking for trouble. So how do they start? Luckily, this is one subject I can give you the facts about, as all is revealed in the story of young Albertus, the fireless, fearless dragon.

Most dragons only lay one egg at a time. If you could see the size of those eggs, you would know why. Occasionally, they lay two. Very rarely, two baby dragons hatch from the same egg.

What happened to Maralu, the mother of young Albertus, is very rare indeed. First of all, she laid two eggs—a feat in itself. Like most dragons, she didn't sit on them or anything, but she made sure they were in a warm, dry cave, where mountaineers wouldn't stick pick-axes into them and geologists wouldn't carry them off. Dragon eggs, you see, look very much like large boulders. I once saw one in a very posh person's garden. It had been carried there from overseas and it looked very fine. I wondered very much what would happen when it hatched!

Hatching, like many things with dragons, takes years and years. Most dragon mothers sleep through this time, conserving their strength for the years ahead when they will have to look after one or more difficult little dragons.

Maralu's two eggs lay snugly in her cave, next to the sleeping mother, for over ten years. Then, one fine spring morning, Maralu woke up feeling a little hungry. She dashed off at once and luckily found a couple of maidens wandering aimlessly in a meadow nearby. We needn't go into the details. It is enough to say that Maralu had a good breakfast and the maidens wander no more.

Back in the cave, Maralu prowled around her eggs. She had a feeling that something was about to happen and she was right. The largest egg began first. It started to rock, ever so gently.

Under Maralu's watchful eyes, the egg rocked faster and faster, until it bashed into the smaller egg. Like a chain reaction, this egg, too, began to rock. Soon both eggs were jiggling about in a completely extraordinary way. They juddered and they shuddered. They jiggled and they joggled. Then, very suddenly, the largest egg went *crack!* with tremendous force. Even Maralu jumped back in alarm.

A large piece of shell fell away from the top of the hatching egg. Out of the hole popped a cheeky little face.

Maralu hurried across to her baby. He looked adorable. But Maralu's shocks were not over. Just as she was about to lift him out of the egg, another little face popped up beside him. This one was even more adorable than the first, and it was a girl. Maralu's heart went thuddedy-dong. (Sorry, I haven't told you about dragon heartbeats. The point is, she was delighted.)

Maralu helped her two little ones out of the egg. They were perfect. They had all their little claws and scales, just as they should. They were not, of course, breathing fire. Maralu bent down and very, very gently blew into their tiny noses. It was a bit like lighting the gas. At once, little flickering flames and puffs of smoke came out. Two more little dragons were breathing fire and not scorching their nostrils at all.

Maralu was so delighted with her little ones and the surprise of having twins that she didn't notice what was happening to the other egg for an hour or two. When she did look up, she saw that it was still rocking, but the rocking was becoming less vigorous. It was as if the little creature inside was finding it just too exhausting to crack his egg. Even as Maralu watched, the rocking stopped completely. The egg sat there and just quivered ever so slightly.

Maralu was concerned. She knew that being able to get out of an egg was a good first test for a young dragon. Little ones who couldn't manage that were likely to have a difficult life. Sometimes, so the old dragons said, it was kinder to leave an unhatched egg and let nature take its course. But Maralu, filled with warm feelings for her new family, couldn't do that. She hurried forward and used her claws to break open the egg. *Crack!* The shell fell apart, leaving a little dragon body panting on the floor of the cave.

This little dragon was certainly not as vigorous and robust as the other two, who were already jumping up and down around the cave and playing leaptail over their mother. But the new little one looked up at Maralu and gave a grateful little smile. The dragon mother's heart melted. She scooped the baby up into her arms and took him off to a corner of the cave where the other two wouldn't jump on him.

The new baby soon began to look better. He stretched and yawned. Then he sat up and began to take an interest in what was going on around him. Maralu was delighted. He looked like a clever little chap. If he wasn't as big and strong as her other children, it didn't matter. Maralu bent down and blew gently into the little one's nose to light his flames.

Nothing happened.

She blew again.

Still nothing.

A little frightened now, Maralu blew harder still.

"Ouch!" said the little dragon.

Maralu tried to think reassuring thoughts. She would try again in a couple of hours, when the little one was on his feet. It would be okay. Still, she watched her son anxiously as he hopped over to play with his brother and sister.

Maralu had had a long time to think about names for her little ones. Two boys'

names and two girls' names (as she only knew that there would be two babies, not three) were ready and waiting. Maralu called the twins Magnus and Agnes. The smallest baby was called Albertus.

Over the next few days, Maralu tried several times to light Albertus's flames. It was no good. His little nose grew sore at her attempts. In the end, it seemed cruel to keep trying, but Maralu was deeply worried.

How would her son cope when it was time for him to go out and find his own maidens to munch? No one, surely, would run screaming from a dragon with no fire and smoke belching from his nostrils?

As the little dragons grew up, they turned out to have different characters and strengths. Agnes was strong and fierce. She chased little mice and frogs all over the mountainside when she was still quite small—and she caught quite a lot of them. Magnus was quieter and more timid. He didn't chase anything at all until he suddenly found that with his long legs he was even faster than Agnes. Then he tore around at high speed. He didn't catch anything, but Maralu was sure that his burst of speed would stand him in good stead.

Albertus was different. He wasn't very strong and he wasn't very fierce. He couldn't run fast enough to catch anything, but he was incredibly brave. When he was still very little, he saved his whole family from a mountain lion—by roaring.

"Well, I didn't know what else to do," Albertus explained later. "He was just standing there, looking at us, and he was much fiercer than us, so I simply charged towards him and roared. I was hoping he would run away. I don't know what I would have done if he hadn't."

"But he did," said Magnus with admiration. "You frightened *him*. It was brilliant, Bert."

"Don't call him that," said Maralu sharply. "It's not dignified. Always remember, my dears, that dragons have a long and distinguished history. We have to uphold the honour of our ancestors."

None of the children had the first idea what she was talking about, but they said, "Yes, Mamma," and trotted off to play as usual.

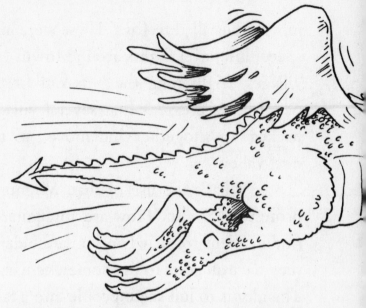

Teenage dragons are just as difficult as teenagers of any other species. Poor Maralu had a terrible time restraining Agnes' tendency to eat anything that moved (including hay wagons, which did her digestion no good at all). It was just as difficult trying to persuade Magnus to keep still for a moment. When he discovered his wings, Magnus found another area in which he could be speedy. He specialized in what he called fly-bys. These were high speed, low-level flights around towns and villages, frightening the wits out of the people to the extent that several villages packed up altogether and moved to the next valley.

"What's the use of that, Magnus?" protested Maralu. "How are you going to find maidens to eat when you are older if they have all gone to live somewhere else? The idea is to lull these people into a false sense of security by sleeping for a few years, then dash out and make a raid when you feel really hungry. It's worked well for dragons for hundreds of years. Now you have everyone so jittery they don't let their maidens out of their sight. Last month I had to make do with sheep, and it's not the same at all. I know all this is just boyish high spirits, but you are old enough now to be more responsible."

"Yes, Mamma," said Magnus, but he didn't mean it. A few days later, however, he caught his claws in a washing-line and almost came to a very nasty end on a furious farmer's wife's pitchfork. After that, he calmed down a good deal.

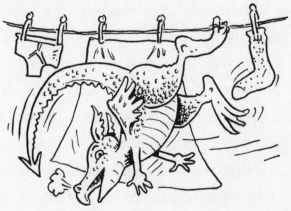

At last the day came when Maralu had only one more thing to teach her babies. Then they would have to go off and find caves of their own.

"Agnes, Magnus, Albertus," she said, "today I will teach you the art of catching and eating maidens. Then you will be grown-ups and can look after yourselves. Now listen carefully."

Maralu explained about the great importance of surprise, the use of smoke and fire in quelling excessive struggling and screaming, the advisability of eating heads first, so that there was no more screaming when you got to the trickier bits, like feet. She warned of the sharpness of coronets, if they were lucky enough to find a princess. She advised against attacking any maiden in armour (which many of them were wearing these days) because of its unfortunate effects on the teeth. She explained that it was simply not done to eat children or old ladies, however hungry you were, but any female between twenty and forty-five was fair game. The rules had been relaxed a lot since the olden days. She warned against feelings of mercy and sympathy.

"It's a slippery slope," she said. "You let one go and you'll start doing it all the time. Everyone knows that dragons eat maidens. It's part of nature. You can't interfere with nature. Now, let's go out and put all this theory into practice."

The four dragons set off together, down to the watermeadows beside the river. There were quite often maidens mooning about down there, picking flowers or combing their hair.

By chance, conditions were perfect. Three perfectly edible maidens were wandering about separately in the water-meadows, which at this time of year were far from watery. Wildflowers bloomed among the grasses. It was an idyllic picture.

"Now," hissed Maralu, "remember, if you do enough with the fire and flames, there won't *be* any screaming. Terrify them enough, and they'll drop down in a faint. Maidens do that sort of thing. Then everything is much easier for everyone. As for you, Albertus, I'm afraid you'll just have to try your roaring trick, but I'm very much afraid that you may have to go without maidens. Give it a try, though. Some of those maidens are frightened by spiders and worms. A great big dragon might just be terrifying enough without flames and smoke."

The three young dragons trotted off obediently. Then, just as the first maiden noticed them coming, they leapt into action. Magnus and Agnes got to their maidens first, of course. They did the full fire and smoke thing, but they did it a little too vigorously. In seconds, the whole meadow of dryish grass and flowers was alight. The maidens screamed and ran towards the river, hurling themselves in with a great splash. The dragons hopped about in frustration. Their nostrils may be fireproof, but their toes are not.

Dragons, of course, hate water. They live in mortal dread of putting their flames out. Albertus, however, did not. He slithered into the water with the grace of an over-sized otter and had eaten the three maidens before his brother and sister had stopped hopping up and down.

After that, Maralu had no fears for her youngest child. He was brave. He was resourceful. He was clever. The fact that he wasn't fire-breathing hardly seemed to matter. Maralu gave a huge sigh of relief (setting several trees alight) and turned her attention to her more unruly twins. Clearly, more work was necessary *there*.

Mr. Majick's Menagerie

Long, long ago, people couldn't travel about as easily as they can today. There were no cameras, so they couldn't see pictures of other parts of the world. There was no television either. Most people didn't have many books with pictures. In those days, there were no zoos, where you could go to see animals from different

parts of the world, but one or two very rich people kept menageries. These were private collections of animals, brought at great expense by expeditions sent out to find them. One man who owned one of these menageries was called Mr. Majick. His menagerie was different from the others in two ways, as you will hear.

For a start, Mr. Majick's menagerie was a travelling one. Each group of animals had its own colourfully painted wagon, with "Mr. Majick's Marvellous Menagerie" painted on the side. The menagerie toured from town to town. Everywhere it went, people queued to see animals they had never seen before. There was a very old elephant, who was rather temperamental. However, she was so much bigger than all the other animals, or Mr. Majick, or his assistant Karlo, that she pretty much ruled the show. If she didn't want to come out of her wagon one day, then she didn't come out. If she didn't want to go back into her wagon, then she stayed outside, and the menagerie didn't move on for another day ... or two ... or in one cold winter ... seventeen.

In another wagon, Mr. Majick had two grumpy camels, an ostrich with a bad habit of kicking camels, and a very large tortoise. None of these animals liked each other very much but they all enjoyed dry, warm living conditions, so they were stuck with each other.

Mr. Majick's third wagon contained a zebra, a miniature pony, a giraffe and a llama. All of these were the best of friends.

Next in line came Mr. Majick's bird wagon. He had several parrots, a black swan, a dodo (remember, this all happened a long time ago), a peacock and a penguin. The penguin used to live in the next

wagon, with the seals and the walrus, but there was such squabbling over fish that he had to be moved.

Mr. Majick also had a wagon full of snakes and other crawling things, a wagon with dogs who did tricks and a wagon containing a young and rather boisterous hippo, whose manners were not yet fit for display to the public.

The wagons described above were drawn by patient old horses, so used to their jobs that they didn't need drivers. There was also a large wagon for Mr. Majick himself and a smaller one for Karlo and his wife.

All of these wagons, as you can imagine, drew crowds wherever they went. Mr. Majick was always careful to make camp near a lake or stream, so that the animals could drink and those that wished could splash around. He once lost a walrus completely, only to find it again the next year when he returned to the lakeside. The walrus was tired of catching his own fish and gladly rejoined the famous menagerie.

I mentioned earlier that Mr. Majick's menagerie was special for two reasons. The second reason is what this story is really about.

Mr. Majick enjoyed his animals very much. He liked them all, even the grumpy camels, and he looked after them as well as he could. But he was much more of a collector than he was a showman. He kept his ears and eyes open, always eager to acquire more animals. As the years went by, a grizzly bear, an armadillo and a rather irritable lion joined the menagerie. But Mr. Majick wasn't satisfied. He wanted something amazing. He wanted something so extraordinary that the whole world would want to come and see it. He wanted his menagerie to be known from Texas to Timbuctoo.

One summer, Mr. Majick found himself travelling in Canada. His animals loved the countryside, lounging by the lakes and playing hide-and-seek (they hid, Mr. Majick did the seeking) in the forests. From a business point of view, it wasn't very successful. There were vast distances to cover and not many people living along the way. Mr. Majick was beginning to think coming so far north was a mistake when he met someone who was to change his life for ever. Her name was Marvela Mireille.

Mr. Majick met Marvela Mireille in a town on a great river. Her clothes were black and her face was always shaded by a large hat and a veil. Among the three farmers and six little boys who formed Mr. Majick's audience one afternoon, the dark lady could hardly escape notice. She lingered when the others left. Mr. Majick hurried forward to find out more about the mysterious visitor.

"Allow me to introduce myself," he said, bowing low. "My name is Morgan Majick. I am the owner of this menagerie. Whom do I have the honour of addressing?"

"Enchanted," said the lady with a hint of a foreign accent. She stretched out a black-gloved hand and gave her name. "I think, Mr. Majick," she went on, "that I have information that may interest you. Interest you, that is, if you are considering extending your menagerie."

"Always, dear lady!" said Mr. Majick cheerily. "I am delighted to hear of interesting new animals. I must say, I did wonder, as we were coming along, whether in these deep forests…"

"Indeed," smiled Marvela Mireille. "There is much that is unknown still. But the animal I am thinking of is very well known. It is simply very rarely seen. So rarely, in fact, that many people think it is mythical."

Mr. Majick's eyes almost popped out of his head. "You don't mean…?" he said. He couldn't bring himself to say the word in his mind.

"What?" asked Marvela Mireille, clearly determined not to help him. She looked steadily at the showman.

Mr. Majick began to feel a little silly. He hardly liked to say out loud what he was thinking. On the other hand, his strange visitor was clearly not going to speak. Mr. Majick prepared to make a fool of himself.

"You don't.," he said eagerly, "mean a *unicorn*?"

Marvela Mireille roared with laughter. She threw back her head and hooted with derision. Mr. Majick felt wounded to the core. He should, he thought, have been more sensible. A unicorn indeed!

But Marvela calmed herself. When she looked at Mr. Majick again, her eyes were gleaming.

"I can see we are fellow spirits," she said mysteriously. "No, not a unicorn, I'm afraid, but something almost as fine." She leaned forward and whispered two words in Mr. Majick's ear.

Mr. Majick was not so discreet. "A dragon!" he cried. "A real dragon? You can't mean it?"

"Oh, but I do," replied Marvela. "Why don't you come with me?"

"Wait just a moment, please," said her host. He called to Karlo and told him to take care of things. He would be away for an hour or two.

"No, no," said Marvela Mireille. "I'm afraid it will be longer than that. My home is two days' journey from here, deep in the forest."

Mr. Majick gulped. Despite his life on the road, he wasn't really a great traveller. Not without his large and comfortable wagon, in any case.

"We will travel in my carriage," said the lady, as if reading his thoughts. "It is not so bad, if the weather stays fine."

"Well, it *is* summer," laughed Mr. Majick. Marvela Mireille gave him a strange look.

"Perhaps," she said.

Before he had time to think about this, Mr. Majick found himself being led to a large black coach with four black horses. His own animals watched as he rattled away, waving his hat from the window.

Marvela Mireille's coachman looked after them well. The first night, he brewed coffee over a fire for them and produced bread and cooked meats from a box. Mr. Majick tucked in with enthusiasm. The lady merely toyed with a piece of bread.

"It's lucky the night is warm," said Mr. Majick. "I can wrap myself up in my cloak by the roadside. Once again, the lady looked at him oddly. There was almost a smile on her face, but it was hard to tell through the veil.

The next day, the party continued on its way. The road through the forest was darker now, and trees seemed to crowd in on every side.

"I suppose it is the shade of the trees that makes it feel so much colder," said Mr. Majick, shivering.

"Perhaps," said his hostess, shrugging her fur wrap closer around her shoulders.

The second night, the coachman made a huge fire, which he kept burning all night.

"It is wise, in these parts," he said.

Mr. Majick, huddled in his cloak, was still cold. He was glad when morning came and they could rattle on their way again, although the coach was hardly warm inside.

"We shall be there by nightfall," said the lady, seeing him shudder, "if the snow holds off."

"Snow?" Mr. Majick looked out of the window. Sure enough, a few large flakes were already falling. "But it's July!" cried the showman.

"Perhaps," replied the lady.

Mr. Majick's thoughts were in a whirl. It had been mid-July when they set off, and they had only been travelling two days. Or was it three? Suddenly, Mr.

Majick wasn't sure of anything any more. How many nights had they stopped on the way? His head swam. He stared out at the whirling flakes and found that he could no longer even see the trees that pressed close to the track.

As he stared out of the window, Mr. Majick felt the road start to climb. The horses went slower and slower. At last, the carriage came to a halt. Mr. Majick was surprised to see Marvela Mireille gather her cloak around her.

"We walk from here," she said.

Outside, the snow was still swirling. Mr. Majick had to concentrate hard and walk fast to keep up with Marvela. He dared not lose her in the snow. He feared he would be lost for ever.

"Hold on to my cloak, if you like," said the lady, again seeming to read his thoughts. Mr. Majick felt like a little boy holding his mother's hand to cross the road, but he did as she suggested.

After a very long time, Mr. Majick saw a dark shape looming up in front of him.

"Here we are!" cried the dark lady, throwing back her veil. And for the first time, by the light of a lantern hanging above the door, Mr. Majick saw her face. Marvela hastily pulled her veil back, but not before Mr. Majick had seen the terrible marks of burning that scarred one side of her face. At almost the same moment, he heard, deep in the earth below him, a roaring sound that chilled his blood.

"We keep him in the dungeons," said Marvela Mireille. "It is the only safe place we have."

For the first time, Mr. Majick felt that he had made a dreadful error. He had read about dragons, of course, but the stories were set in the time of knights and ladies. They hadn't seemed real. It had never occurred to him that dragons could be dangerous. It was hard work looking after a geriatric elephant and two grumpy camels, not to mention an untrained hippo and a greedy penguin, but as long as they were well fed and well cared for, they tended to have more sense than to bite or scratch or stomp on Karlo and Mr. Majick. The elephant had, it was true, once sat on a warthog with disastrous results, but that was only unfortunate for the warthog. The lion stayed in his cage and was no kind of problem. Mr. Majick had once been kicked on the bottom by the ostrich, but he had only hurt his dignity. But a dragon! A fierce dragon! Was it possible to keep it safely? Was it possible to show it to the public safely? Frankly, there wasn't much point in having it if it couldn't be shown.

"I'm wondering," said Mr. Majick, "whether I have been a little foolish in coming with you. Maybe a dragon isn't ideal for the kind of menagerie I have. It could be that I have made a mistake. If so, I'm sorry for wasting your time."

"Come with me," said Marvela Mireille. "You can't really judge until you have seen."

Mr. Majick followed her down some grim stone steps. The roaring grew louder and louder.

"There!" said Marvela Mireille. "What do you think?"

She stood aside, and Mr. Majick found himself staring through thick iron bars into a massive dungeon. Staring back at him, his red eyes gleaming and great flames leaping from his nostrils, was the dragon. It really *was* a dragon.

Mr. Majick looked at the dragon. The dragon looked back. Then it opened its mouth and roared so loudly that the stones in the walls shifted in their places.

Mr. Majick's head filled with fear, but his heart filled with something else. He felt enormous pity for the dragon. In that roar had been all the horror of being shut up for year after year, unable to fly, unable to roam the forests and the high mountains. The dragon's red eyes were filled with a sadness so deep that Mr. Majick felt tears forming in his own eyes.

"This is monstrous!" he cried, turning to face Marvela Mireille. "How dare you keep him here like this? Let me take him with me now!"

"Perhaps," said Marvela Mireille, "I will add to my own collection instead."

"What do you mean?" asked the showman, feeling his courage drain out of his boots. He could no longer see the lady's face, but he knew now what it looked like.

"I collect *people*," said the lady. "You would fit nicely into my collection. Would you care to see?" And she flung open another door, through which Mr. Majick could dimly see grey figures chained to the walls.

Mr. Majick shut his eyes. He prayed that he was dreaming. When he opened them again, Marvela Mireille was still there, but the open door seemed to have disappeared.

"So," said the lady, "you may take the dragon now." And she flung open the iron gates to the dungeon and fled up the stairs and out of sight.

Mr. Majick suddenly felt very calm.

"Come," he said, and walked before the dragon out of the castle.

Outside, it was a clear, cold night. Mr. Majick turned to the dragon, who was breathing in the sweet night air in great gulps and stretching his wings in joy.

"If you will take me home," said the showman, "then you can go free."

The dragon lowered his head as if in agreement and spread his wings again. Mr. Majick, hardly believing that this was happening to him, flew on the dragon's back, swiftly and silently, to the camp near the river where his own wagons waited.

The animals were still. Karlo was asleep. Only the rushing of the river could be heard.

"I will take these animals back," said Mr. Majick, "to where they belong, if it takes me the rest of my days. Now you must go, too. Hurry, before it gets light!"

For a moment the air flamed gold and orange as the dragon breathed his thanks. Then he was gone, flying through the night towards the mountains.

Mr. Majick sighed. The air felt warmer here, and the chill had gone from his bones. He shook his head. Had it all been a dream? And he thought he heard the voice of Marvela Mireille.

"Perhaps…"

Treasure Trouble

Dragons love to collect treasure. It is one of their main pleasures in life. There is nothing a dragon loves more than to see a huge pile of treasure glinting and gleaming in the light of his fiery breath. Gold, silver and jewels are the most prized possessions. A dragon learns at an early age to detect fakes and cast them aside. Indeed, many a prince has been mortally offended to find that a dragon has raided his treasure-house and *left some things behind.* Dragons are some of the most discerning thieves in the world. At least, most of them are...

Not so long ago, a young dragon called Mildu was sent by his mother to his uncle to learn about the right way to go about acquiring treasure. Uncle Walpu was only too happy to put his nephew through his paces. His own collection of treasure was second to none.

The first part of the teaching was on the theory of treasure-seeking. Uncle Walpu dealt with methods of gaining entry into vaults, dungeons, banks and strongrooms. He explained how locks could be opened with claws and teeth or, failing that, by melting with a dragon's breath. Mildu proved an eager pupil.

Next, Uncle Walpu talked about the safest ways to carry treasure away. This can be tricky for a flying dragon, but wherever possible, dragons find a bag or net to put the treasure in. Mildu made practice flights holding rocks and branches, until he was quite confident.

"Remember," said Uncle Walpu, "if it's a choice between taking treasure or being able to make a safe getaway, leave the treasure behind. You can always go back for it another time. It really is better to be safe than sorry."

Mildu nodded wisely. There were a few more practice runs, in which the young dragon had to decide how much to carry. Finally, Uncle Walpu declared that he was satisfied. It was time for his nephew to go out on his first raid.

"There's a castle near here where a miserly old duke keeps a hoard of gold," said Uncle Walpu. "It's easy to get in and out, and the old man is too mean to keep many security people to protect all his property. You shouldn't have any trouble. Keep your wits about you, and bring back something nice for me, too!"

Mildu flew off, feeling nervous and excited. Back in his cave, Uncle Walpu paced up and down. He hoped that the young dragon would be successful this first time. He didn't want his confidence to be damaged. The mission should really pose no problems, but one never knew with a young dragon. They could lose their heads in a crisis.

But Uncle Walpu need not have worried. Within an hour, Mildu was back, carrying in his claws a big bag bulging with treasure. Uncle Walpu's eyes shone as he greeted his nephew.

"Any problems, lad?" he asked.

"It was easy," said Mildu. "Everything was in a big building outside the castle. I didn't have to go anywhere near the duke himself. And just look what I've got!"

Saying this, Mildu opened the big bag he had dumped on the floor. Uncle Walpu looked eagerly at the shining objects that clattered and spun on the floor of the cave. He couldn't believe his eyes.

"Mildu!" he cried, "what have you done? These are ... these are... *hub caps*!"

It was true. Rolling around the floor were twenty shiny hub caps. Rolls Royce hub caps. Mercedes hub caps. But hub caps all the same.

"Why," asked Uncle Walpu faintly, "did you bring these?"

"They're shiny," said Mildu. "Aren't they treasure, then?"

Uncle Walpu counted to eighty. He reflected that he had clearly missed out on teaching young Mildu some of the basics. It was back to theory for them both. It had never occurred to the older dragon that his nephew would need to be taught to recognize treasure when he saw it.

Three weeks later, after an intense course on hallmarks and gems, Uncle

Walpu felt that Mildu was ready once more. He had taught him all he knew about jewels, gold and silver. Surely, now, the lad was ready.

Once again, Mildu flew off, this time at night, to the castle with the miserly duke and the fleet of unused cars. Sadly, things did not go according to plan. The theft of the hub caps had, of course, been discovered. The duke, fearing quite rightly that the liberating of hub caps might be followed by the theft of something a good deal more valuable, updated his security system. He now had half a dozen men with dogs patrolling the grounds, while a

state-of-the-art alarm system was installed in the castle itself.

Now alarm systems, even state-of-the-art ones, do not usually assume that break-ins are going to happen from the air. Mildu landed on the roof without being detected. A little breathing on the lead of the roof, and Mildu had made a hole large enough for any dragon to get through. He clambered into the attics of the castle.

Mildu's plan had been to sneak all the way down the main stairs to the cellars, where he understood that most of the gold and silver was stored. It had not occurred to him that there would be anything worth stealing in the attics. But Mildu was surprised to see lots of square, shiny things stacked in a corner. He didn't know that these were gilded picture frames, or that the very odd-looking pictures of old-fashioned people in the middle were old masters and very valuable. He was simply taken by the shininess of the frames. Yes, Uncle Walpu had schooled Mildu long and carefully that all that glitters is not gold. He had instructed the young dragon always to look for a hallmark and, if possible, a maker's mark as well. But all this went right out of Mildu's head as soon as he saw such big golden objects. He felt sure that they must be worth something. And they weren't attached to any kind of car, so that must be good.

Mildu tied as many of the pictures as he could together with some rope he found in a corner. Then, clutching the rope with his claws, he launched himself

from the hole in the roof.
Unfortunately, the young
Mildu's rope-tying skills
were about as good as his
treasure-recognition skills.

As he flew over the castle
courtyard, one of the smaller paintings
slipped from the bundle and fell down,
down, down to the flagstones below. As
the picture passed the topmost windows
of the castle, the famous state-of-the-art
alarm sensors were triggered. A horrid
noise of bells and sirens filled the
air, frightening poor Mildu
half out of his wits.

A second later, he was
caught in the glare of
dozens of powerful
searchlights criss-
crossing the
grounds.

Now security men and women are used to some pretty strange sights, but a flying dragon is not one of them. They stood, open-mouthed, looking up at the apparition above them. The duke himself came running out of the castle and looked up as well. Coming as he did from a long

line of dragon-fighters (admittedly a very long time ago), he was less stunned by the sight than the security personnel.

"Shoot it!" he cried.

Mildu had no idea what this meant but he recognized a mean and vicious voice when he heard it. He pulled himself together and remembered Uncle Walpu's words. Dropping the bundle of pictures, he headed off towards the mountains as fast as his wings could carry him. The big pile of pictures, dropping like a stone, hit the unfortunate duke squarely on the head, putting an end to his miserly days and not doing a lot of good to the pictures in the process.

Back at his cave, Uncle Walpu was almost knocked off his feet by Mildu's hurried and inelegant landing. He didn't need to be told that things had gone badly wrong for his nephew.

It took Mildu some time to pant out his story. It took Uncle Walpu even longer to work out what had really happened, for Mildu knew nothing about searchlights and talked about monsters with big eyes instead. He didn't understand about alarm bells either, but said that the monsters had horrible shrill voices that shouted.

From all the confusion, Uncle Walpu picked out what was, to him, the only important point.

"What you stole, or tried to steal, Mildu," he said severely, "were pictures. Look at me, now. Are they on the list I made for you of the ten most desirable items of treasure?"

"No," said Mildu miserably.

"Are they even on my list of the hundred most desirable items of treasure?"

"No."

"So why did you steal ... try to steal them then?"

"They were shiny," said Mildu, hanging his head.

Uncle Walpu completely lost his temper. "Windows are shiny!" he roared. "Bald heads are shiny! But should you try to steal them? NO! It is so simple, Mildu, that even a human could understand it. Gold, silver and jewels. Silver, gold and jewels. Gold, jewels and silver. It doesn't matter which way round you say it. There are only three things worth stealing. What are they?"

"Sold, jilder and gewels," said Mildu unhappily. At which his uncle gave a sigh that set fire to several trees three miles away and flapped off into the night to cool his temper in the moonlight.

It was clear that returning to the castle would not be a good idea. When he felt calmer, Uncle Walpu sat down and wrote out a plan for his nephew's further education. It was very detailed. It included lots of time for repetition and revision. It covered things so basic that most dragons would have been ashamed to have them pointed out. It was at just the right level, however, for Mildu. Uncle Walpu vowed to stay as calm as he could and prepared to do his duty.

Frankly, it was hopeless. Mildu appeared to grasp everything in a classroom situation, but as soon as he tried to put the theory into practice, things went disastrously wrong. His attempt to steal a shiny weather vane demolished the tower of a local church. His visit to a local bank left him locked into the vaults, from which he was rescued in the nick of time by Uncle Walpu. When he attempted to raid a jeweller's shop, he returned home with five huge imitation ingots made of plastic, which unfortunately had huge imitation plastic hallmarks on them.

After each disaster, Uncle Walpu took a few days off to regain his shattered composure. During these times, Mildu wandered idly around the mountainside, paddling in the cold, clear streams and amusing himself by kicking the rocks to create small avalanches. When one of these avalanches threatened to block up the entrance to Uncle Walpu's cave, while Uncle Walpu was inside it, Mildu was told not to go outside until he was given strict instructions on how to behave. The young dragon wandered around the network of caves instead, kicking at the walls and sighing heavily.

Uncle Walpu persevered for six months. He did everything he could. He even flew himself on treasure-seeking missions with Mildu, despite the fact that it is an unwritten dragon law that two dragons do not fly around together. After all, a human being might persuade himself that he was halucinating if he saw one dragon in the sky, but two dragons take a lot more explaining.

Of course, side by side with his uncle, and with his uncle's voice talking him through every step, Mildu was fine. He could steal even the trickiest items when he had that kind of support. The problems came when the young dragon was let out on his own. Without some kind of guidance, Mildu went to pieces. He didn't think. He didn't plan. He didn't use his head at all. He had a fatal weakness for anything shiny, however unsuitable it was. At long last, even Uncle Walpu, who prided himself on his teaching skills, had to admit defeat.

"Mildu," he said, "I am going to send you back to your mother. It breaks my heart to let her down, for she has been relying on me to teach you all I know. But I must draw the line somewhere. I've spent so much time with you in the last few months that my own treasure-store has hardly grown at all. I've done all that I can for you. I'm afraid that you will never have treasure of your own and that is the end of it."

Mildu hung his head.

"I'm sorry," he said. "I have really tried hard. I guess I simply can't get all these difficult techniques into my head. I just can't understand why gold and silver and jewels found the easy way don't count as treasure."

"What are you talking about?" asked Uncle Walpu wearily. "What easy way is there?"

"Why, collecting the treasure that is just sitting in the mountains, waiting to be found, of course," said Mildu. "Look, I'll show you!"

He led his uncle deep into the cave and kicked at a wall. Several glittering objects fell to the ground or sparkled in the wall. They were diamonds! Outside, Mildu showed his uncle the little nuggets of gold he had found in the streams and piled up behind a convenient rock.

For several moments, Uncle Walpu was speechless. Then he smiled.

"If I was wearing a hat, I would take it off to you, young Mildu," he said. "Of course this is real treasure, and why we dragons go flying about risking burglar alarms and guards with guns when all this is here, I can't imagine. I really don't have anything left to teach you. Tell your mother she should be proud of you and go straight home."

"Couldn't I just stay a few more days?" asked Mildu.

"Certainly not!" laughed Uncle Walpu. "The diamonds and gold on this mountain are *mine*!"

The
Flightless
Dragon

Many baby birds have to be taught how to fly by their parents. If they are reluctant, a little push from a high branch usually does the trick. The little birds start flapping by instinct and before they know what they are doing, they're flying! If only it was as simple as that for baby dragons...

Many a dragon mother has, I'm sure, been tempted to take her offspring up the mountain to a handy precipice and give him a hearty shove. Unfortunately, with dragons, it's just too big a risk to take. Dragons are not light and feathery, like birds. They are large and scaly. They need to develop considerable strength in their wings and shoulders before they can fly. If you pushed a baby dragon off the top of a mountain, I'm afraid there would not be much of him left to be scraped up in the valley below.

Almost as soon as they have hatched, little dragons are given exercises to do by their mothers. That is exactly what happened to Plodlu.

"*Rotate* those shoulders!" called his mother. "Let me see your muscles working, Plodlu! One, two, three, four! *And* the other way. Four, three, two, one! And *up*! And *down*! Now one more time!"

Poor Plodlu was not an athletic young dragon. He was a sitting-down-by-the-fire kind of dragon. He didn't take naturally to all this effort. But he did wiggle his shoulders a little to show willing and tried to copy his mother.

After several days of these special strengthening exercises, Plodlu's mother moved on to wing extensions.

"*Stretch* those wings!" she cried. "Out, in, out, in ... *all* the way, Plodlu! Well, move away from the wall then! Now, again! One, two, out, in, three, four, out, in!"

Once again, Plodlu struggled, but he could tell by his mother's tone of voice that this was important, so he did his best.

A few weeks later, Plodlu's mother took him outside and made him jump up and down while flapping his wings.

"Feel that lift!" she shouted, landing rather heavily herself. "Up, down, up, down, that's the way! Not too near the edge now!"

Plodlu tried to feel the lift but all he really felt was silly. Here he was, a plump and rather clumsy young dragon, heaving himself up and down like a forkful of mashed potato. He couldn't get the wing and jump sequence right for a start. He was always lifting his wings as he jumped, which his mother said was wrong.

"No, no, no!" she yelled. "*Down* with the wings and *up* with the legs. Stop, stop! That's not right. Now, legs first. Up, down, up, down. Now add the wings ... down, up, down, up. Oh dear. All right, pick yourself up and let's start again."

Plodlu's mother hadn't expected to be doing quite so much exercise herself while teaching her little one to fly. But while she got fitter and fitter, Plodlu got more and more confused. Pretty soon, his mother had him doing practice take-offs along a broad, flat ledge on the mountainside. He had to run along, flapping his wings and getting faster and faster until, for a few short steps, he was gliding through the air.

"Faster, Plodlu! Faster!" cried his teacher, thundering along behind. "Don't forget to flap!"

But Plodlu simply couldn't do both things at once. If he remembered to run faster (and it seemed that acceleration was pretty important), then he forgot to flap his wings. If he remembered the flapping, he simply jogged along at a pace that wouldn't have got a feather into the air, let alone a rather solid dragon. Plodlu's mother tried to think of enticements.

Next morning, when Plodlu woke and wanted his breakfast, his mother smiled and said, "Well, it's up on that big rock at the end of the ledge. Run along, flapping, and you'll be able to jump up and get it."

Plodlu loved his breakfast. He went outside and began trotting along the ledge with rather more enthusiasm than he had

before. But he found that thoughts of his waiting breakfast put him off completely. He couldn't flap and run and think about breakfast at the same time. In fact, he couldn't do anything and think about breakfast at the same time. Thirty seconds later, Plodlu's mother heard a plaintive cry and came out to find her son clinging by his claw-tips to the edge of the ledge. His acceleration had improved, but his sense of direction hadn't.

After that, Plodlu was too frightened to try running along the ledge again. His mother took him up to the top of the mountain, where there was a flat, grassy plateau, just right for a learner.

Plodlu ran and ran and ran. But no matter how much flapping he did, he didn't take off.

"It's co-ordination again," sighed his mother. "If only you had a little more sense of *rhythm*, Plodlu. Just a minute, I've got it!"

Plodlu's mother stomped off and came back with a very old wind-up gramophone that she had liberated from a wealthy duke some years before. She wound the turntable and heard the sounds of a delightful waltz wafting across the plateau.

"There you are, Plodlu!" she cried. "Just copy me!"

And with a *one, two, three, one, two, three, one, two, three*, she was off, whirling and twirling, sometimes on the ground and sometimes in the air. It looked pretty good.

Plodlu listened hard to the music. He set off, feet flying and wings flapping, around and around and around … until he was sick. His mother turned off the music with a sigh and carried him home. Clearly, more work needed to be done.

Over the next few weeks, Plodlu's mother showed a great deal of inventiveness. She made him several exercise machines from branches and rocks she found lying about. Using this equipment, Plodlu did find himself getting stronger. He lifted his dumb-bells, practised his sit-ups, and stepped up and down on to several big rocks until he could lift, sit and step no more. Even his mother was impressed.

"You're shaping up nicely, Plodlu," she said. "Now all we have to do is to put your exercises into practice. It's time for some real flying. You have the strength now, you simply have to learn the skill."

Plodlu felt a lot more confident with his new muscles. He even skipped along as his mother led him to a grassy slope on the other side of the mountain.

"Now," she said, "all you have to do is to run down the slope, flapping as hard as you can, and you'll soon find yourself in the air."

Plodlu looked down at the slope. It was fairly steep but there was no horrible precipice at the other end. He took a deep breath, stretched out his wings, and set off. Faster and faster, Plodlu flapped and ran. His little legs twinkled along the ground. His little wings could hardly be seen, they moved so fast. Halfway down the slope, could it be? *Yes!* Plodlu had taken off! He was flying! Er ... no, wait, what...? Plodlu's mother rubbed her eyes. What on earth was the boy doing? He couldn't be, could he? As Plodlu swung around towards her, she was sure. *He was flying upside down!*

Plodlu's mother sat down on the grass and hid her eyes. She had never, ever heard of a dragon flying upside down. It could only end in disaster. It did.

Plodlu, unable to judge the steepness of the slope, crash landed. Naturally, as he had been flying upside down, he crash landed on his head. A dazed and confused young dragon lay on the grass.

"Plodlu, sweetheart, are you all right?" cried his mother, bending over him tenderly.

"Lollipops," said Plodlu distinctly. "Lollipops and gravy."

Clearly, he was suffering from serious concussion if not something worse. Plodlu's mother gently carried him home and put him to bed in their cave. It was several days before the young dragon was himself again, and even then he had a lump on his head that took weeks to go away. It seemed cruel to pursue the flying lessons when he was poorly.

While she looked after Plodlu, his mother had time to think. Would her son

always be so hopeless at flying? What would be the best way of keeping him safe in the future? The more she thought about it, the more the older dragon was forced to come to the conclusion that the safest thing would be if Plodlu never flew again.

A dragon who cannot fly? A flightless dragon? Plodlu's mother turned these phrases over in her mind and felt deeply uneasy. She had never heard of a dragon who could not fly. Her Great-Uncle Nobu, who lived a long way to the east, had injured his left wing once. It never was any good for flying after that. But Great-Uncle Nobu had managed very well with only one wing. For a long time, he could only fly in circles, but after a while, even that was sorted out. But not flying at all? That was a different matter, and one that worried Plodlu's mother a great deal. Night after night, she sat by her son's bedside and worried.

As it turned out, Plodlu's mother was worrying about the wrong thing. As soon as Plodlu was better again, he was eager to get back into the air.

"It was great, Mum," he said. "I really enjoyed the flying. I don't know why I went upside down. It just sort of happened. What I need is more practice."

Reluctantly, his mother took him out to the grassy slope once more. This time, she covered the slope with leaves and hay so that if (she thought it was more likely to be *when*) Plodlu came heavily to earth, his landing would be cushioned. She was right. Plodlu crashed several more times, each time hurting a different part of his body. In the process, he perfected upside-down flying, sideways flying, loop-the-looping and sky-diving. He looked remarkably graceful in the air. It was just the landings that were lacking.

"Perhaps if I landed on water," he mused one day.

His mother was horrified.

"No, Plodlu!" she cried. "You know perfectly well that water and dragons don't mix. If you manage to put your flames out, it will be no end of trouble to light them again. It's too big a risk to take."

Even Plodlu could see the sense of this. But he really didn't like crashing into the ground quite so often. Then, one evening, he had a brainwave.

"I've got it!" he told his mother. "I know how to stop hurting myself!"

"Practising your landings?" asked his mother. "Or giving up flying entirely?" These days, after nursing Plodlu through two broken legs, a badly twisted elbow and a dislocated knee, she was open to any suggestion. But she was not ready for what Plodlu said next.

"If I stay up in the air all the time, there won't be a problem," he said airily. "My difficulty is landing. The solution is not to land. I'm surprised I didn't think of it before."

"But…" said his mother. "I mean, how…? I mean, that's ridiculous! You can't just stay up there! You'll get tired!"

"Not if I glide," said Plodlu. "I can stay up for ever if I just glide and rest. I can even sleep when I'm gliding. I had a

little go this morning. The thermals around the top of the mountain are really strong. There's no danger at all."

"What about food?" asked his mother faintly. "There isn't anything to eat up there, unless you're going to start munching birds, and I've never fancied feathers, myself. Surely you're not going to do that, Plodlu? You'll need to eat to keep up your strength, sweetheart!"

"You could throw my meals up to me," said Plodlu calmly. "I'm so good at aerial acrobatics now, I wouldn't have any trouble in catching them. Then, when I'm a bit older, I'll practise seizing maidens on the wing. It should be pretty easy with the element of surprise. By the time they know what's happening, the silly things will be breakfast."

"But what are you going to do all day?" asked the poor mother dragon. "Won't you get bored, just flying around?"

For Plodlu's mother, flying was a purely parctical matter. A dragon flew, she thought, in order to get from A to B. She didn't understand the pleasure her son got from gliding and zooming, twizzling and turning. It all seemed very strange to her.

Plodlu was laughing. "I won't be bored at all," he chuckled. "I'll be so busy building up my business, I won't have time to wonder what to do."

"Business?" Plodlu's mother felt she had come into the plot several pages too late and couldn't grasp what was going on.

"Yes," said her son confidently. "I'm going to run a dragon aerial acrobatic show. We should get lots of spectators. And they may like to pay in food, too, you never know."

"But there are only a handful of dragons for miles around," said Plodlu's mother. "You'd only ever have an audience of about three, although I, of course, will always come and watch you."

"Not dragons," explained Plodlu, "*humans*! They're the ones with spare maidens to eat and buns to throw."

At this point, Plodlu's mother, who had been feeling faint for some time, fell with a crash to the ground. This time it was Plodlu who had to do the looking after for a while. He knew why his mother was worried. Dragons and humans have not, traditionally, got on well together. Dragons profess not to understand this. It doesn't seem to occur to them that visits involving stealing treasure and munching maidens are not occasions of joy for the human world. Humans have no particular interest in seeing the better side of dragons either. They have several excellent legends about heroes who have bravely slain any dragon who crossed their paths. It would be unfortunate if they ever found out that most dragons are pussy-cats underneath. They are gentle, kind, funny and friendly (but they do enjoy the odd maiden for breakfast, it's true).

Plodlu's mother did her best to talk him out of his plan, but he had made up his mind. Perhaps you have heard of the flying dragons of China? The rolling dragons of Afghanistan? The tumbling dragons of Japan? The cloud dragons of Peru? They are all a single dragon, of course—our old friend Plodlu. And where

Plodlu goes, his poor old mother is sure to be found skulking behind a nearby hill.

So that is how a dragon with very poor flying skills, who looked at one point as though he would never fly in his life, became the famous flying dragon we all hear so much about. It just goes to show what determination can do for you, but I wouldn't advise that you try it at home yourself. We simply don't have the wings for it.

The Dragon's Egg

Wizard Wazoo was in trouble. In fact, he was in the deepest trouble of his terribly troubled life. Ever since he was a small wizard, learning at his father's knee, he had made mistakes. A mistake in your maths homework can be a problem. It may incur the wrath of your teacher or your parents, but it doesn't turn them blue or make your house dissolve. Wizard Wazoo's mistakes did things just like that. It was very fortunate that his father was a wizard as well, because most of the time

he could put things right without too much trouble. Sadly, the older wizard is no longer waving his wand in our world. These days, Wizard Wazoo is on his own. These days, Wizard Wazoo is in trouble more often than he is out of it. And even his cat, Carlaminda, can't help him.

The particularly bad trouble that I mentioned at the beginning of this story came about because Wizard Wazoo was fond of strawberries. Being a wizard, he didn't see why he should have to wait until summer to enjoy his favourite fruit. A little bit of wand-waving here, a sprinkling of magic dust there, and *hey presto!* … straw. Ooops.

As is often the way, what had started as a mild wish for strawberries became desperate as soon as there was difficulty in obtaining them. Wizard Wazoo fixed his wizard stare on the pile of

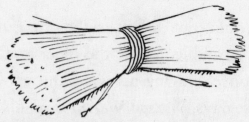

straw. He clenched his wizard teeth and muttered his wizard words. *Da DA!* In a second the straw turned into a pile of cranberries.

Cranberries are all very well in their way. They make a refreshing drink. They go well with turkey. But they don't do anything for a wizard with a requirement for strawberries. Wizard Wazoo rolled up his sleeves. He got out his most powerful wand. He cleaned out his second-best cauldron and started to make a berry-bringing brew. It contained snails, slug-

slime, used tea-bags, peppermint foot lotion, orange peel and one or two other ingredients that you would probably prefer not to know about. Wizard Wazoo stirred and murmered. Carlaminda, seeing the green steam rising steadily from the cauldron, ran under the bed and stayed there with her head in her paws.

Soon, the green steam turned to blue steam. The smell became very bad indeed. The bubbling of the mixture seemed to take on a life of its own. Wizard Wazoo looked back at his spell book, its most popular pages spattered with past potions. He checked his ingredients, read the instructions, turned over two pages at once, and made the fateful mistake of saying the magic words backwards.

There was silence for a long moment, during which the only sounds were the sluggish bubbling of the mixture and the whimpering of Carlaminda, who had a pretty good idea of what was going to happen next. Suddenly, it was as if three brass bands and a road-drill had squeezed into the room at once. Everything that could clatter clattered. Everything that could bong bonged. The glasses tinkled. The windows twinkled (loudly). Wizard Wazoo's teeth chattered and he had a very strange feeling, as if someone was trying to turn him inside out. Then there was a puff of orange smoke, a clash of cymbals (or possibly saucepan lids) and the house zoomed into the air and headed for Siberia.

Wizard Wazoo shut his eyes until the house landed. He didn't have to look out of the window to know that it was very, very cold. Shivering and shaking, he relit his fire and pulled his cloak around him. He had to work out how to get home. And the worse thing of all was that his craving for strawberries had not stayed at home. If there was one single thing that Wizard Wazoo knew about Siberia, it was that strawberries were remarkably thin on the ground.

Five hours later, although the fire was roaring under his second-best cauldron, Wizard Wazoo had icicles growing from his toes. He found it terribly hard to concentrate on his spell book when he felt so cold. He had skimmed through all the easier spells at the beginning of the book, hoping to find something he could adapt. Nothing was suitable. Even the fairly-hard spells in the middle of the book, which Wizard Wazoo only attempted on his better days, were no use. The freezing wizard was forced to look at the very difficult spells towards the end.

The last section of the book had pristine white pages that had never been touched by a wizard's potion-spattered fingers. They advised on many problems that Wizard Wazoo hadn't even known existed. His eyes opened wider and wider at each page he turned. "How to tame a wild brontosaurus" had three pages of ingredients and such a complicated set of instructions that Wizard Wazoo couldn't even understand the first one. "How to open the packaging on supermarket cheese sandwiches" seemed to require a level of wizardry that Wizard Wazoo had no hope of ever acquiring.

The poor wizard, whose feet felt like ice and whose fingers really *were* ice by now, had almost given up hope when he turned the last page and saw "How to send your house back home from Siberia and find strawberries at the same time."

With mounting excitement, Wizard Wazoo read through the list of ingredients. Toenail clippings—yes! Marmalade—yes! Cucumber face cream and a pink sponge—yes! Lawnmower oil—yes! Sixteen-day-old pea soup—strangely enough, yes! Two holly leaves—yes! The longest quill of a bad-tempered porcupine—yes! Three jars of pickled onions—yes, yes, yes! A dragon's egg—oh... It was the very last ingredient, and poor Wizard Wazoo knew perfectly well that he didn't have one. He looked vaguely around the frosty room, but he knew it was hopeless. Dragon's eggs are big. They're not the kind of thing you could miss. Wizard Wazoo crouched over his fire and tried to think.

At that moment, Carlaminda, who felt she couldn't bear to stay in Siberia a moment longer than was necessary, crawled out from under the bed and curled around Wizard Wazoo's all-too spindly and shivering legs. She pointed her pretty paw delicately at the word "dragon" and waved elegantly at the window. Wizard Wazoo looked at her blankly.

Carlaminda gave a sigh of deep-felt exasperation and hurried over to the book shelf. She pulled down a magazine with her teeth and carried it over to her master. Wizard Wazoo looked down at the brightly coloured cover. "A new magic cloak in a weekend!" he read. "My wife's a warlock!" screamed the cover. "Free with this issue two packets of super spells!" it went on. "Siberia: undiscovered land of magic and mystery!" it finished, and there was a picture of a smiling dragon sliding down a snowy slope and waving at the reader with both hands.

Wizard Wazoo peered at the picture. Then he tried to open the magazine to read the story inside. It wasn't easy with frozen fingers, but at last he found the page. It seemed that Siberia was trying to attract more holidaymakers and had decided to target the readers of *Magic Monthly*. One of the attractions, he read, as well as the bracing climate and the soothing scenery, was the Drooski Dragon Park, where real live dragons could be seen in their natural environment.

In no time at all, Wizard Wazoo had pulled on his extra-thick hiking socks, wrapped his neck in a moth-eaten scarf, and pulled his wizard's staff from the pot where it had been holding up an unhealthy looking plant. He threw open the door, letting in blasts of snow and frozen air, and plunged out into the wintery wilderness beyond. Then he hesitated, staggered back into the room, picked up a protesting and squirming Carlaminda and tucked her under his cloak.

The conditions outside were truly atrocious. Wizard Wazoo hunched his shoulders and tried to think himself warmer. In this he was, surprisingly, quite successful, although Carlaminda doing her own magic under the cloak may well have helped a good deal.

Gradually, as the wizard struggled on, the weather improved. The blizzard stopped and the sun came out, almost blinding Wazoo with its brilliance. It was hard to know which way to go, but as luck would have it (and Wizard Wazoo was not renowned for his acquaintance with luck) he spotted a large sign ahead. "Welcome," it said, "to the Drooski Dragon Park. Entrance: 12,000 roubles."

Poor old Wizard Wazoo didn't have one rouble, never mind 12,000. He was about to sink down into the snow in despair when he realized that there was no one at the gate to take his money. He had happened to turn up at just the moment when the gatekeeper went off to have his seven-hour lunch. Feeling slightly guilty, Wizard Wazoo slipped through the gates and into the park, picking up a leaflet from an open box as he did so.

Wizard Wazoo had (temporarily) learnt his lesson as far as reading useful instructions was concerned. He stopped and conscientiously read what the leaflet

had to say about not feeding the dragons and trying not to disturb them when they were sleeping. There was also a section entitled: "Safety Note". It was not very encouraging. "If attacked by a dragon," it said, "try screaming. If that doesn't work, you will have nothing more to worry about … ever."

For the first time, it occurred to Wizard Wazoo that he should have brought his book of spells with him. It also crossed his mind that perhaps mother dragons were not madly keen on complete strangers coming and stealing their eggs. Thirdly, it came to Wizard Wazoo that a dragon's egg, as well as being large, might be very heavy. Could he remember enough magic to get it back to his snow-bound house? Wizard Wazoo was not much of a wizard at the best of times. Now, he felt every simple carrying spell he had ever known slip silently out of his head. All I need now, he thought glumly, is to meet an irritable dragon.

"Ahem!" A voice behind him made the wizard wheel around like a Cossack dancer. His worst nightmare had come true. Standing before him, not six feet away, was the biggest dragon he had ever seen. In truth, he had never seen one at all in the flesh before, and he found now that magazines gave an entirely misleading impression of their size. And this dragon didn't just look irritable. She looked out and out *furious*.

"About time too!" said the dragon in fluent Wizard. "Come on, come on, let's not hang around here. It's freezing. Even with my fire-breathing, I find this climate intensely annoying. Are you coming or not? Well?"

Wizard Wazoo looked bemused. "What?" he stuttered. "Where?"

"To find an egg, of course," said the dragon crossly. "I don't have one myself at the moment, but my neighbour is terribly careless with hers. She won't even notice if we borrow one."

As if in a trance, poor Wizard Wazoo followed the dragon through the snow. When they came to a hillside, she told him to wait and disappeared into a cave. A couple of minutes later, she emerged, holding something that looked like a very large boulder.

"I can't carry that!" cried Wizard Wazoo. "I couldn't even lift it. Oh no, whatever am I going to do? I wish I hadn't ever said that spell this morning. Why didn't I listen to everything my poor old father told me? I'm a total failure as a wizard. Oh dear!"

"Have you quite finished?" asked the dragon coldly. "You don't have to carry the egg, do you? I'm doing that. And as for the rest, it's past caring for."

She stomped off across the snow with the egg, pausing only to check that Wizard Wazoo was following her. Inside the wizard's cloak, Carlaminda kept very still. She had an uncomfortable feeling that she might make a tasty snack for a dragon.

When the unlikely pair reached the wizard's house, now almost covered with snow, the dragon gave a big sigh.

"This place is hopelessly small," she said. "Do something about it, will you?"

Wizard Wazoo gaped. "M-m-make it bigger, you mean?" he asked.

"Well, I certainly don't want to be smaller," said the dragon witheringly. "Come on. It's a pretty simple spell, I believe. Round about page 18 of your spell book, I think."

The wizard almost panicked, but just in the nick of time, the spell came floating into his mind. A few swift words and a tap on the door with his wizard's staff, and the house kind of shook itself and grew to about double its previous size. It was still a bit of a squeeze for the dragon to fit through the door, but she squeezed in and dumped the egg on the floor.

"Come on," she said, "get on with the spell, will you?"

"You're coming, too?" asked Wazoo, trying and failing to imagine the dragon in the quiet suburb where he lived.

"Of course," said the dragon.

On reflection, Wizard Wazoo realized that there was absolutely nothing he could do about it. He concentrated on the spell instead. It certainly taxed all his powers. Once or twice he felt sure that he had gone wrong, but at last all the steps were done and it only remained for the final word to be said. Wizard Wazoo said it.

In a flash, a breeze of warm air wrapped around the house. There was a shaking and a sound of breaking. Then the house, still much larger, was back in Wizard Wazoo's garden. And on every surface there was a large bowl of strawberries.

"But why did you help me?" asked a relieved Wizard Wazoo, gazing in wonder at the dragon.

"For the strawberries, of course," she said. "Take your hands off that bowl right now!"

The Last
Dragon

Charlie Keddle sat under his favourite oak tree and read his favourite book. It was about animals in danger and he found reading it a bit sad, but Charlie was an optimistic boy and he hoped that there was something that could be done to help all these animals. Charlie was particularly interested in endangered animals because his father was a zoologist and was even now in the darkest, deepest rain forests of Brazil checking on the numbers of various creatures threatened by things that people had done. Charlie was very proud of his dad and hoped to be a zoologist himself when he was older.

On his bedroom wall, Charlie had a map of Brazil with a big pin in it just where he thought his dad might be. He also had lots of pictures of animals around the room. And each night, when the first bright little star twinkled through his

small bedroom window, Charlie wished that he could go to the darkest, deepest rain forests of Brazil and help his dad.

One day, much sooner than he had expected, Charlie got his wish. But it wasn't at all in the way that he wanted. He was sitting at the kitchen table, drawing a big picture of a parrot, when his mother went to answer the telephone. When she came back, her face was white and she leaned against the table as if she was finding it hard to stand up.

"What's the matter?" asked Charlie. "Is it Granny?"

Charlie's granny had had something wrong with her for as long as Charlie could remember. Every time he saw her, she sighed and told him that she might not be much longer for this world. Charlie's mum was not very sympathetic.

"Nonsense, Mum!" she would say. "Stop frightening him! You're as fit as I am and you know it."

Now Charlie's mum shook her head. "No, it isn't Granny," she said. "It's your dad. You must be a big, brave boy, Charlie."

"He isn't...?" Charlie couldn't bring himself to ask the question. He could hardly bear to think about it.

"No, no," said his mother. "But he hasn't come back from his latest expedition on time and they haven't heard from him for over a week. There's no reason why anything should be wrong. He might have had trouble with his radio or something. But they're going to send a party out to

look for him, just in case he's hurt or lost somehow. We must try not to worry."

But it was very hard not to worry. Charlie knew that his dad was always very careful when he went on an expedition. He believed in taking sensible precautions. He knew about the dangers of the rain forest and he did his best not to take risks of any kind.

"It won't do the animals any good if I fall into the river and get eaten by those vicious little piranhas," he used to tell Charlie, laughing.

Charlie knew that his mother was finding it hard to manage, too. She kept forgetting what she was doing and staring out of the window. Every time the phone rang, she jumped and snatched it up. When, as usual, it was Granny, with another complaint about her bunions or her reading glasses, Charlie's mum could hardly manage to be polite.

"It's not her fault," she told Charlie after one very tense call. "I haven't told her about your dad, so she doesn't know anything is wrong. I thought it was best not to worry other people until we know something for sure."

Charlie hoped his granny wouldn't keep bothering his mum, and she didn't. She arrived on the doorstep the next morning with a suitcase and a determined expression on her face.

"You may think I'm stupid, Sarah," she said briskly, "but I'm not. I can tell something is wrong even from fifty miles away. I think you're worried sick about something. I also think you should tell me about it and see what I can do to help. You're not so old you don't sometimes need your old mum."

Charlie's mum burst into tears and hugged Granny. Then they all had coffee together at the kitchen table and talked about what had happened.

"It's clear to me that you should both be there," said Granny. "I know you probably can't do anything to help, but you'll feel better being on the spot. And when he is found, as I'm sure he will be, you won't have to wait before you see him. Let's find out when the flights go."

Sarah Keddle tried to protest, but her heart wasn't in it.

"I'll stay here and feed the dogs and the cat and the wallaby and whatever that creepy thing in the bathroom is," said Granny. "You just go and get ready. Everything will be just fine when all three of you come home."

Twenty-four hours later, Charlie found himself in an ancient Jeep, rattling down a dirt road towards the camp where his dad's colleagues waited for news. He looked out at the forest all around him. Even from the Jeep, he could see that it was teeming with life. When he actually set foot in it himself, he was astonished. The rain forest seemed to be more alive than anywhere he had ever been. You looked at a leaf and it would suddenly open its wings and fly away. You saw a

twig and it would scuttle off to the forest floor. Birds chattered in the trees. Brightly coloured frogs jumped up into the branches. It was a magical place. If only he could have been there under different circumstances!

For three days, Charlie and his mother waited for news from the search party. On the fourth day, as they sat under canvas and tried to keep cool, they heard a shout from the edge of the forest. It was the search party returning.

"Oh, please," whispered Charlie's mum, clasping her hands together.

The pair rushed eagerly across the clearing, but the returning men looked tired and defeated.

"There was no trace," said the leader. "We could see where he had been working, and we found his radio and his compass, but there was no sign of him at all. We stayed until our supplies were low. There's still a chance, of course, that he'll make it out by himself."

There was a "but" in his voice. The boy and his mother knew that the chances were getting slimmer with every day that passed. That night, as Charlie looked up at the starry sky, he had more than his fair share of wishes. There was only one thing in the world he wanted now. He was very much afraid that it was the one thing in the world he could never, ever have.

The next day was filled with waiting again. And the day after that. As the sun slipped up over the trees on the third day, Charlie couldn't bear it any more. He ran out of his tent and into the forest. He had decided to find his dad all by himself.

"Dad! Dad!" called Charlie, as he pushed through the bushes by the clearing and on into the rain forest beyond. It was quite dark there. The leaves overhead shut out the sun, except for little sparkling patches that splashed the ground with light.

Charlie walked and walked, shouting all the time. When he finally stopped, he was so hungry and tired that the forest seemed to be spinning around him. He crumpled in a heap against the trunk of a giant tree. For the first time, Charlie felt afraid. There was no one to help him if a poisonous snake came along. He knew that he had done something very silly.

As Charlie closed his eyes, a kind voice spoke in his ear.

"Don't worry, Charlie. It will be all right. You'll see."

Charlie looked up into the friendly face of a beautiful dragon. At first, Charlie thought he was dreaming. Then the dragon sighed and little flames flickered around her nose. Charlie could feel the warmth of them on his face. It was real!

"Who are you?" asked the boy. "I haven't seen a picture of you in my book."

The huge creature shook her scaly head a little sadly. Where the sun glinted on her, Charlie could see that her skin was the most beautiful colours—red, gold, blue and green.

"I'm a dragon," she said. "Human beings seem to think we all died out long ago. Well, they are almost right. I am the very last dragon in the world."

"That's terrible," said Charlie. "Isn't there anything I can do to help?"

"Just keep believing in me, Charlie," said the dragon, "and I will still be here. I am living in your dreams. But why are you out here in the forest, all alone?"

Charlie found himself telling her all about his father and the terrible time that had begun with a telephone call just over a week before.

"How awful for you," said the dragon. "But think how worried your mother must be about *you* now!"

Charlie hung his head.

"I know," he whispered, "but now I'm lost, too." He started to cry.

"Don't do that," said the dragon. Tears rolled down her own cheeks and sizzled when they met the flames. "I can help you," she said. "But I can only do so much. You will have to choose. I can show you how to get out of the forest. Or I can help you to find your daddy. Which will it be, little one?"

"Find my dad. Oh, please, find my dad," cried Charlie. The dragon smiled.

"But if I find your dad," she said, "you will stop dreaming and I will be gone for ever. Is that what you want?"

Charlie looked up into the dragon's big yellow eyes and put his arms around her neck.

"I want my dad more than anything in the world," he said. "I'm sorry."

"You don't have to be sorry about that, little one," said the dragon. "I think I can hear him now. Listen!"

Faintly at first, and then louder and louder, Charlie heard sounds of movement in the forest. Then a figure stumbled into the clearing. He was dirty and his clothes were torn. His face was unshaven and thin. But Charlie knew at once who it was.

Daddy!" he cried, throwing himself across the clearing.

"Charlie! What are you doing here? Are we near the camp?" said his dad, giving him a huge hug.

"I'm sorry," said Charlie. "I'm a bit lost, too." But as he spoke, he saw out of the corner of his eye something large and beautiful disappearing through the trees.

"But I think I know the way!" cried Charlie. "Follow me!" He dashed off into the forest, chasing his dream.

It was two exhausted zoologists who stumbled into the camp as the sun went down that night. Charlie's mum was laughing and crying and shouting all at the same time. Much later, after rest and food, no one seemed to want to sleep.

"I suppose you will want to go straight back out there," said Charlie's mum to her husband.

"Those animals still need to be saved," explained Mr. Keddle, "and it can be done."

"Not always," said Charlie softly. He thought about the last dragon, her big, kind eyes and her gentle voice.

"I'll never forget you," he whispered.

There was no reply.